Fire And Desire

By

G.E. Griffin

To Genesis: It was all worth it in the end.

"The rules of fair play do not apply in love and war."

– John Lyly, Euphues: The Anatomy of Wit

1

Nairobi

It was illegal to be at the beach after dusk but here we were, sitting in front of a makeshift bomb fire, my younger sister was lying across my lap. The sun was just about peaking over the horizon. It made it a bit easier to see if anyone was coming down the shore. The West Palm air was salty, and I could smell a storm brewing. The wind blew strongly against the ignited blaze, and I could feel the shiver that ran through Venice's body.

Here we were... back at square one.

Being back on the streets was better than selling my soul to the devil. Running my fingers through Venice's coils, I thought back on our lives and gagged inwardly.

FIRE AND DESIRE

***

"Mommy, stop it! You are hitting her too hard! You'll kill her!" Venice shrieked, pulling at her arm.

Sahara, our mom, turned and backhanded Venice, knocking her aside.

"Now give it to me!" she screamed, kicking me in the ribs.

An *oof* sound rumbled from deep inside me as my vision blurred in and out. I folded myself into a fetal position to coddle my aching body.

"The money is for Venice's field trip, Mom, please stop." I choked, hoping to die, but what would happen to Venice?

"You idiot! Where is it?" she yelled, leaving me to dig through my backpack only to find nothing.

I sighed in relief. I had already paid for Venice to be gone for a week. It would be good for her mental state and mine as well. The only way, however, that Sahara would calm down is if I gave her cash. Luckily, I had some money in my pocket from the night before with Omar.

"Mom! If I give you what I have, will you leave us alone?" I rasped, coughing as I reached into my pocket.

Sahara turned around, almost caught whiplash from how fast her neck turned.

"Give it here!" She snatched 200 dollars' worth of tips from my hands.

Not a glance at fearful Venice, Sahara marched out of the house and into the humid night. Venice ran behind her to safely lock the door shut. I could finally close my eyes and rest.

"Nairobi!"

I could hear my name ring through the fog, but I was already gone.

$$***$$

"Robi?"

Blinking back into reality, I looked down at a concerned Venice staring right back up at me.

"Robi? Are you okay? I was calling your name for the longest time, and you weren't answering me," she said, tugging on one of my wicks.

"Of course, I'm okay. I'm with my favorite person in the world, why wouldn't I be okay?" I asked rhetorically.

"Okay… if you're sure."

"Yes, I am sure, silly goose."

Venice smiled, but I knew I wasn't off the hook due to her inquisitiveness. She continued to lay in my lap, allowing me to keep playing with her coils. I couldn't help but smile too. It was hard not to.

Although she was still a baby, to me, my sister was beautiful. We share the same smile and big brown eyes, but her expressions were still full of life. Those orbs held nothing but innocence, despite all that we've gone through as children. Her big kinky hair that I loved so much was blowing in the salty air. Venny hated wearing her hair up because it was a task to detangle.

My sister was model material; the total opposite of me. Where I was short and stubby, she was tall and slim. She still had some time, and I was excited to see her at her full potential.

I hate that she grew up so fast, though. I would never wish that on any child. I wish I could take away even just that little piece of damage our dysfunctional life has brought upon her.

She always knows when I'm thinking about our past—our parents and Omar. I wish our lives could be better than this.

"So, what did you want to tell me?" I asked, slowly working a knot loose with my fingers, feeling the hair grease gathering under my fingernails.

The scent of the Frenchie grease was strong, but something about the smell always reminded me of the woman I remembered my mother to be. Despite our circumstances, I chose to reminisce on how close we once were. My mother wasn't always an alcoholic, but when that man left us, everything just fell apart. No one really knows why he left... he just up and vanished. What made matters worse, he took everything and left us with just the house. At the time, all mom had to do was tend to the home, and I was the only one bringing in money. I can remember when there was nothing to worry about. But now, it's all I do.

"Oh yeah..." she murmured, her voice trailing off as she grew distant.

"Hey, tell me."

"What will happen since I haven't been going to school? I am glad we left Omar's house, but while I was there..." She slowed, allowing me to connect the dots.

I sighed internally. It had been a few weeks since we left Omar's house—pimp house, to be exact—and that was our stability. I could remember clearly how he threw us out, our belongings dumped on the curb. I can still feel the eyes of the other women he owned, staring at me with eyes of both sorrow and envy. I understood both emotions, but all I could think about was where Venice and I were going to be after this.

Now that everything had settled, the realization of how this was affecting Venice was starting to hit me. She had a life before this catastrophe, and I cannot be the one to hold her back from being a child. Looking at our bags, we needed to get out of this weather before we were caught in the storm.

"C'mon! I have a surprise for us tonight," I said, changing the subject and helping Venice up.

"Where are we going?"

"It's a surprise," I grinned, wiggling my eyebrows and whispering.

She laughed. "Okay, let's go."

***

The Winners Palm Beach is one of the local's finest hotels, and I have always wanted to spend two nights there, at least, and tonight's the opportunity to do so. The place was glorious. Built near the ocean, you could still smell the salt in the air. I knew this would lift our spirits.

"Robi? What is this place?" Venice asked in awe.

"This is our surprise, Venice! Did you know that it is scientifically proven that humans need a good night's rest before going to school? For the next two nights, we will be here. I know it is temporary, but I figured… why not?" I explained, pulling the strap of our duffle bag tighter against my shoulder.

"By the looks of it, this is an amazing surprise! Thank you, Robi." Venice giggled, pulling us the rest of the way to the door.

I laughed, letting her pull me along. From the outside, it looked like a Spanish villa, colored in erosion cream. It was hard not to awe at how high the arches of the building were as we made our way into the prestigious lobby. I could not believe how nicely this place looked for its affordability. The hotel was bustling with many upper-class and maybe even middle-class folk. Hand in hand, we walked up to the front desk to the clerk, and by the look on her face, I knew she felt like we didn't belong.

That's okay. I thought. *Ain't nothing gonna stop me from getting a room here tonight.*

"Good evening, my name is Kasey. How may I assist you? Looking for a room for the night?" She asked, giving our appearance a sweeping glance.

Usually, I'd be mortified, but given our circumstances, I could care less about what Kasey or anyone else felt about my appearance.

"Yes, we are. For two nights, please. We would like a suite," I replied, shifting my weight because the duffle bag was beginning to put a strain on my shoulder.

"Would that also include breakfast?" she asked, sounding bored as she rolled her eyes.

"Yes, thank you," I answered, finally deciding to put the bag down, ignoring her attitude.

"Okay, that'll be $1,390. Credit card," she said, putting her hand out, still not acknowledging that I was a person.

Venice's eyes nearly bugged out of her head as I reached down into our bag and pulled out a little pink case that held our most valuable possessions. I could hear the receptionist mumbling, but I refused to pay her any mind. I squeezed Venice's hand, reassuring her that everything was okay. She was getting antsy, and honestly, so was I. We both were tired and ready for a real bed. Just as I was about to hand her my card, a masculine hand came into my vision, stopping the transaction.

"Can you—"

She was interrupted by a strong, fortifying voice. Turning towards the deep and raspy sound, I was taken aback by the beauty in my personal space. He matched the profile of a chocolate Adonis. A strong stallion. He was gorgeous, and I was speechless.

"Don't worry about her payment. It'll be on the house."

Kasey tensed, her fingers pulling away from my debit card. "Yes, sir."

"Um, no, sir. I can pay my own way. Who are you, anyway?" I questioned, stepping in front of Venice to block her from view.

"My name is Raphael Pierre, the owner of this hotel. It's my duty to make sure all my guests are well taken care of."

His eyes held an unexplainable intensity that had the power to enslave its captive, but I refused to fall under his spell.

"Kasey, give these ladies the Atlantic suite facing the ocean."

Taking in his appearance, I noticed his flawless skin. His lashes were long and full, his lips looked… edible, as I watched them give out orders. Kasey and I both gaped. *Facing the ocean?* I opened my mouth to decline, but there was a tug on my shirt; looking at me were the pleading eyes of Venice. My shoulders dropped in defeat.

"Thank you. You did not have to do that," I said, reaching for my bag.

Raphael quickly took the duffle bag from my hand, leaving no room for protest, and handed me the room keys instead. "Well, I wanted to. There is nothing wrong with helping someone, even if they can do it on their own," He said with a wink, handing the room keys to a peeking Venice. "Now let's get you and princess to y'all room. You guys can stay as long as y'all like."

Venice smiled brightly, showing off her chocolate gums and pearly whites. Smiling in return, Raphael led the way, with Venice in pursuit. I sped up to keep up with their pace.

My eyes widened. *Stay as long as we like?!*

"Thank you, Mr. Raphael Pierre. Also, is breakfast part of the deal?" Venice asked cheekily.

Mr. Pierre chuckled beautifully, "Well, of course, and you can just call me Ralph. Let's not forget there is dinner, too, if you're hungry."

"I'm starving! Do y'all have meatloaf? That sounds amazing right now!" Venice was getting ahead of herself.

"Venice! Where are your manners?" I said, a little taken aback by how quickly she'd gotten comfortable. We'd just met the man, and she was already too cozy.

"Sorry, Robi, but I am starving, and Ralph said they got all we can eat! We should make the best of it while we are here, right?"

I wanted to protest but I knew she was right. I was tired, and food did sound good right now. Almost on cue, my stomach growled.

"By the sound of Robi's stomach, food is definitely a priority," Raphael said with a grin, giving Venice his full attention. "I'll get our chefs to work on that."

"Awesome! I cannot wait to have some dinner. It's been a while since I had meatloaf and mashed potatoes... don't get me started on gravy, mmm!" Venice practically salivated, squeezing her backpack straps.

"Nairobi," I corrected, trailing behind the pair.

"Excuse me?" Raphael questioned, tilting his head in my direction.

"My name is Nairobi," I repeated.

"I apologize, Nairobi." He made another left, "Here we are."

Unlocking the door, he pushed it open. The smell of lavender and clean linen sheets greeted us, immediately calming my nervous system. Venice rushed in to explore the lavish space. I could hear her joyous laughter filling the room, making me smile, but it didn't last long.

"Thank you, Mr. Pierre. We appreciate it, but why are you doing this? People ain't this nice nowadays." I rambled, crossing my arms under my bosom.

"Let's get inside before we discuss anything, please," he replied calmly, motioning for me to enter while he waited at the door.

Cutting my eye at him again, I moved to one of the sofa chairs, the soft cushions nearly swallowing me whole. I fought my tense muscles against relaxation, but I could tell it was a losing game.

Raphael had allowed the door to shut securely behind him, but kept his distance, standing near the entrance — careful not to block the only way out. It stayed quiet for a while, except for Venice's occasional bursts of excitement from across the suite. Meanwhile, he and I regarded each other with sharp, cautious interest.

Frustrated, I wondered... *What was even his end game? What was there to discuss?*

I could not sense him being a threat to us, but I refused to let my guard down. I took in my surroundings. The room was a sight to take in, spacious and decorated with neutral colors of browns and creams. I couldn't wait until the morning to see the sun shining through the room.

"I want you. That's why," he said suddenly, cutting straight into my thoughts.

What? This man must be out of his mind!

I snickered, rolling my eyes. "Please, you don't even know me."

"I'd like to."

"That's all you men are good for, always expecting something in return. Just selfish..." My voice drifted off as my eyes subtly scanned the room, searching for anything I could use to defend myself if he decided to cross a line.

"I have no intentions of causing either of you harm. Forgive me, I am aware that I tend to come off too strong when it comes to things I want, however, this doesn't change how I feel."

"Whatever, mane. You don't know what you are talking about, let alone feeling." I waved away his words. "Thank you for this, but we won't be here for long. Have a good night, Mr. Pierre." I dismissed myself, leaving him where he stood to search for Venice.

"Good night, Ms. Nairobi," he murmured softly.

The door clicked shut, announcing his departure.

2

Nairobi

Pressing snooze on my phone, I was awake. In fact, I have been up for a while but could not bring myself to leave the bed. I was not sure when the next time we would be able to indulge in such pleasures, so I did not feel bad for sinking deeper into the foam.

Opening my eyes, I peered at Venice's peaceful face, blinking back the tears that threatened. My mind drifted to last night, the way she'd devoured the promised meatloaf, the joy on her face. I shook my head softly.

I promise our lives will not be like this forever.

Getting up, I went through our bags, finding us something to wear. Taking out our toiletries, I sighed. Venice was right, she had to go to school. I wanted to avoid raising any unneeded attention and potentially get Venice taken from me. Allowing Venice some more time to rest, I went to take a quick shower when I heard a knock at the door. Wrapping myself in a fluffy, black robe, I made my way to the door. Standing on my tippy toes, I gazed through the peephole to see a cart of food, as well as 'Mr. Delusional' at the door.

I rolled my eyes, opening the door. "Don't you have workers for that?"

"Good morning, Ms. Nairobi. I was hoping you guys were up for breakfast."

"Morning," I replied, moving out of the way to let him and the food in. "Venny! Breakfast!"

Looking at the man whose eyes were burning holes in my head, I quirked a brow. "So… what's for breakfast?"

Wordlessly, he took the gold metal tops off each plate, revealing an impressive spread — fluffy pancakes, crispy bacon, scrambled eggs, fresh strawberries, and sliced fruit. A small feast.

I could not deny that my mouth was watering at the sight. Smelling the savory-sweet scent, a sleepy Venice appeared, yawning and rubbing her eyes, her wild curls sticking out in every direction.

"Somebody said breakfast?" she sighed, half asleep.

I chuckled, "Yes, baby. What do you want? There are eggs, pancakes, and strawberries, your favorite."

Following Venice, we took a seat at the small dining table, and not far behind was Raphael with the cart. Now fully awake, Venice pointed to everything she wanted to eat, trying everything in sight.

As I got up to make her plate, Raphael put his hand up to stop me. It was unnerving that he was here and now he was trying to take over and I did not like it one bit.

"Mr. Pierre –" I began tightly.

"Nairobi, have a seat, I got it," he commanded, holding my glare.

Gritting my teeth, I kept quiet. I did not want to scare Venice. She has seen enough bickering, and I would not subject myself to it. Sitting down, I knew we were not going to be here for long, so there was no point in trying to take a stance. If Venice is okay, I'm good. I sat docile, allowing him to fix our plates, refusing to acknowledge his efforts as courting but as a form of professionalism.

"Thank you," I murmured, waiting for Venny to have a bite before forking my eggs.

"Really good, Raphael! Thanks!" Venice praised, inhaling another piece of sausage.

"It's no problem at all. How was last night's meatloaf?" Raphael asked, covering the food to keep the heat in.

"Spectacular!" Venice exclaimed excitedly.

Raphael chuckled softly. "I see you've learned a new word!"

Venice cheesed. "Mrs. Bluu is teaching us new vocabulary words for our writing project that's due before summer break. Speaking of Mrs. Bluu, I miss school, Robi! Am I going today?"

"Just as promised!" I solidified, placing my fork down, "When you're done, you can get dressed, and we can be on our way."

Venny whooped, drinking some orange juice.

I smiled, getting up from my seat. "Raphael and I are going to step outside to have a talk. I placed your clothes out for you so when you're done eating, we can be on our way."

"Bet."

Brushing past Raphael, I led the way to the exit and held the door for him, so we would be in the hallway.

"Did you need a ride to Venny's school? I can have my driver take you guys," Raphael offered as soon as the door closed behind us.

"Honestly, Mr. Pierre, I don't know what game you're playing, but I'd appreciate it if you'd cut the act."

Again, those brown eyes molten into mine, this time causing me to shift awkwardly from foot to foot.

"Nairobi, excuse me for my forwardness. This is not an act nor a game. I intend to make you mine."

"I am not interested, Pierre."

"You don't have to be so cold. There is nothing to be afraid of. You are safe, Nairobi."

My stance stiffened, "Excuse me?! Safe?! Do I look like a damsel in need of saving?!"

Raphael visibly bristled, rising to his full height. "You misunderstand me."

Just as I was about to answer, the door opened, revealing a concerned Venice. "Everything okay, Robi?"

Breaking eye contact with Raphael, I turned to my sister, "Yes, everything is okay. I see you are ready. Let me get dressed and we will be on the way."

"Okay." Venice looked between Raphael and me before going back into the room.

"I am sorry for being rude. Thank you, but no thank you," I said, following behind my sister and closing the door behind me.

3

Raphael

Thank you, but no thank you. I could not seem to get those words out of my head. I tapped my pen against the mahogany desk before pausing at the thought. This woman wanted nothing to do with me and it only made me want her more. I would not call it obsession, though.

I resisted the temptation to go after her because something had not felt right. She and her sister, being alone in the sweltering streets of West Palm Beach, made my stomach turn, but I could not force my will on them. That was not my style. The sun was going down and I still had a lot of work to do. If I could do anything right now, it would not be sitting behind a desk for eight-plus hours.

FIRE AND DESIRE

During the day, I make millions in the private sector as a gun distributor while also offering protection services to high-profile clients, and at night I distribute other things that government officials would deem illegal. I also dibble and dabble in cybersecurity. Some would say I have my hands full, but there's nothing like being top dog. I am my competitors' worst nightmare and that made me untouchable. It was my ace in the hole if anyone tried to shake the boat, but I digress.

Just as I was about to begin working out linguistics for the company, there was a knock at my office door.

"Enter," I responded, not looking up from my desk.

"Yo, boss, I got those whatchamacallits you requested," the familiar voice said, gaining my attention.

"Gabe, at some point you gotta start using your words," I replied, looking up and making him laugh.

Gabriel Hernandez was my right-hand man and my best friend. We've known each other since junior high and have been street pharmacists through college. He was my brother from another mother.

"Y'know English isn't my first language, *hermano*," He tsked, placing a few manila folders he had in his left hand on the desk. "These are the numbers I gathered from each district that we currently preoccupy."

"Seems like everything is under control," I hummed, taking my time to flip through each file, satisfied. "Have you heard from Omar?"

"He has not checked in yet. The streets have been talking though, and it seems like your woman is connected."

By this point, Gabe had taken a seat, and his words caused me to straighten up.

"Enlighten me."

"Apparently, she used to work for him, and he kicked her out. She and her sister. Now, we both know how he gets down, so I am sure I don't have to go into much detail, but y'know, I never liked that *Bastardo*."

In his right hand was a single folder, which held information on Nairobi. He handed it directly to me.

My jaw clenched. I did not believe in the mistreatment of women, and I tried to steer clear of any involvement with Omar, but sometimes our interests aligned. However, after hearing this news, there was no way that I was going to continue to implicate myself with someone like him.

"Heard. Any ventures that connected me to him, consider them null and void, effective immediately. What else have you heard about her?"

Opening the folder, there was basic information on her and her family. There was a high school picture of her where she was smiling casually, her wicks were still at their baby stage. She was wearing light makeup, and her full lips were dressed in clear gloss and lined with black lip liner. There was no hiding her natural beauty. The other picture in the file was an old family photograph. I recognized Nairobi immediately, holding an infant that I assumed was her little sister. Flanking to her sides were her smiling parents. They looked happy. The father in the picture looked familiar, but I couldn't seem to put a name to the face. Something was up.

"I could not find anything on her after high school besides the basic demographic. Nairobi Xenos. Her mother was Sahara Xenos. Died recently from alcohol poisoning. A younger sister, Venice Xenos. Hard life for a growing teenager. No known information about their father besides his name."

Sympathy and anger pooled in my belly. It had all made sense why Nairobi's guard was up. This world had not been kind to her, and she was only in survival mode.

Xenos. I pondered. *Why did her last name sound so familiar?*

"See if you can find anything else on them. Check the shelters and nearby hotels. There is a hurricane coming and there is no way I am allowing them to be out in that weather. Get everyone you know on it and make sure to emphasize how important this is," I commanded, ready to get out there and search for them myself.

"You know I got you, *hermano*, but there is something you should know about their father," He trailed off, scanning the files further.

"You know I don't like surprises," I said, itching to know more.

"When I first started digging up info on this chica, her last name gave me a strong case of déjà vu. So, I looked more into her mom, and believe me, I was shocked," Gabe explained, flipping through the files and handing me a document titled "SAMMY X." "The conveniently deceased Samuel Xenos is Nairobi's father."

I sucked my teeth. *Samuel fucking Xenos. It all makes sense now.*

Samuel Xenos, aka Sammy, and I go way back. Before the big bucks, he and I were partners. I made a name for myself on campus, and I thought it was a good idea to bring in some fresh faces. Gabe and I were in our last semester and by this time, the business had grown bigger than I could have imagined. What started out as just selling weed out of my college dorm room had become income to pay my way out of student loans and shit. Things were simple before I met Sammy.

Life always has a way of fucking shit up. My usual connect got busted on some foul shit. Word was, dude had gone down for killing his baby mama. This, of course, made me desperate for a new weed man, hence my new relationship with Sammy.

FIRE AND DESIRE

Young Ralph should have done a better job of vetting him before he became the new connect. During that time, I was getting my degree in business management, and I needed to be able to pay off these bills and stay fed. I could have asked my parents, but I wanted independence. Honestly, I wasn't thinking about making this lifestyle long-term, but the money was getting better, and I was becoming invested in it.

Gabe was going on and on about how Sammy seemed a bit shady but, in my mind, no one in the drug business could be trusted so it didn't really bother me. However, I should have listened to him because I could have avoided a bunch of shit, but I digress.

Anyway, things were going well until he started bringing Omar around. Omar was always doing some out-of-bound bullshit and Samuel was nothing but a brainless tagalong. It was making Samuel sloppy. Product was going missing. Money wasn't adding up. The only new variable was Omar. I tried to tell Samuel about his homeboy, but he wasn't trying to hear it.

One evening, Gabe and I were on the prowl, slinging dope on the outskirts of campus. It was homecoming night, which was the best time because everybody would be out trying to get fucked up. Both Samuel and Omar were on the football team, and they were supposed to play that night, but Omar was nothing but a lousy, manipulative prick. Still is.

FIRE AND DESIRE

***

"Let's hurry this shit up. I ain't tryna miss the game," I said, sliding twenty bucks into a brown paper bag.

"Bet," Gabe replied. "I got about a zip left. What about you, *hermano*?"

"Shit, I just sold my last dub. We'll split the rest with Sammy and O. We deserve a lil reward for all our hard work," I winked.

He laughed, throwing his arm around my shoulder, and wagging his finger at me. "Great minds think alike. Let's bounce. Lucia is waiting on me and I can't disappoint."

I laughed.

Making our trip back to campus, we rode our bikes to the old McDonald's nearby. The building was up for renovation and wouldn't be open until next year. Gabe and I usually took this way as a shortcut. Locking our bikes to the bike rail outside the fast-food joint, we could hear shouting. The sound of scuffling was getting louder as we got closer to rounding the corner before that familiar booming filled the air. Looking at Gabe for confirmation, I reached into my waistband. Peering from the side of the building, my eyes widened in shock. Samuel and Omar standing over a body.

"Next time, you'll mind your business," Omar sneered, reaching down to grab a small plastic Ziploc bag.

If I didn't make a move now, that man would be dead soon.

"Gabe, call the cops," I moved from my hiding place. "The fuck is y'all stupid ass niggas doing?"

Samuel, spooky ass, jumped, nearly dropping the gun.

"Oh shit, Ralph. Wassup playa! The game ain't start yet?" Omar grinned. "Just handling some unfinished business."

"Sammy, this what we doing now?" Ignoring Omar altogether. "Running around here being an errand boy?"

Gabe came and flanked my side, giving me the heads up that help was on the way.

"Wassup Gabe," Omar greeted, smiling.

Gabe uttered something unintelligent under his breath but stayed quiet.

"It was self-defense. He was tryna rob us."

"You just threw your whole life away."

Omar laughed. "Nigga, you his daddy? Samuel is a grown-ass man."

"Ain't nobody talking to you, bitch-ass nigga," I said, eyes locked on Samuel. "I hope you know what the fuck you're doing."

I could hear the faint breathing of the dying man a few steps away from me and the sirens coming down the street.

"You called the cops?" Samuel shook visibly.

"You think I'm the only one who can hear the gunshot?" I asked, mock incredulous. "Today must be the Fourth of July."

Omar scoffed, bringing the attention back to himself. "Snitch. Let's go, Sammy."

Just like a lackey, Samuel ran off with Omar. Not wanting to be at the scene when the police arrived, Gabe and I left as well. Later that night, news headlines read: *"BLACK MAN FOUND DEAD BEHIND HBCU."* We also lost the homecoming game.

***

"What do you want to do, *hermano*?"

After some contemplation, I leaned back into the chair. What was I to do? I wanted her, but it was evident that our future was doomed. Looking at her smiling picture, I ran my hand down my face.

Fuck it.

"This doesn't change anything. The plan stays the same. Just keep me updated."

Gabe laughed, nodding his head, "You are one crazy *Puta*, but, okay. *Ya hablamos.*"

I shrugged my shoulder, *"Ya hablamos, hermano."*

FIRE AND DESIRE

***

"Papa?" I picked up the call on the first ring.

"Poukisa mwen pa wè ou? Eh?"

No form of greeting. Just straight to business. I would not say all Haitian folk are like this, but with my family, showing love was not easy. It is not that we do not love each other, but it was instilled in our culture to be strong in every sense. There was no downtime to be soft, hence my default to indifference. I was not born on the island, and I haven't experienced what most have, but culture is culture.

"Dad, I have been working, you know that."

"Manman ou vle wè ou. Make sure you come home soon."

"Okay, Dad."

There was no point in arguing with him. In fact, I had no choice. Forget the whole "planning" part, driving down to Miami was just how it always went.

This was how our conversations always went: him calling, telling me to come home, and me saying I would. Don't get me wrong, going home wasn't the issue. Being single and childless was.

Every time I go home, I know my mom will be expecting me to have my wife on my arm. She's ready to become a grandma, and my father wants whatever she wants.

What she does not know is that the type of life I live doesn't allow me to keep people close. I want a family, but I am too deep in this lifestyle, and it would be selfish of me to involve someone as important as a wife and children. I am so careful that my life back home is nothing but a fantasy. Those drives to Miami are nothing but casual business. Period.

Thank you but no thank you. The words whispered through my mind again.

She was right to deny me. I am a selfish man, and I am not willing to give up living a double life to settle down. She didn't know me, but she read me like an open book.

I shook her from my thoughts and focused on the conversation with my Dad, answering only when necessary until he was satisfied he had done his job by getting me home to Miami.

"Dad, listen, mwen bezwen ale, men map rele ou pita." I said, ready to end the call and to get back to business.

"Don't make my bouch long, okay? I will be expecting you."

"Yes, sir," I conceded. "Bye, papa."

"Okay!" he huffed, ending the call, "Bye!"

I leaned back into my seat again with a sigh of resignation.

Dade County, here I come.

4

Nairobi

The sun was shining, but its heat was non-existent. By luck, Venice and I were prepared for the wind. Honestly, I wasn't trying to panic, but I wasn't sure what we were going to do once the storm struck. I tried not to think about Raphael and the possibility of still having a warm place to stay.

"Robi, where are we going?" Venice's stomach growled. "I'm hungry."

Tears pricked at my eyes. "We are almost at the shelter, love. I'm sure they'll have something for us to grub on when we get there."

"Okay."

We were currently trudging through the strong, brisk wind and if my feet were aching, I was sure Venice's feet were taking a beating as well. She wasn't a small child anymore, so there was no carrying her on my shoulders. I held tightly to Venice's hand, afraid that I'd lose her to the harsh winds.

"Do you think Mommy will let us come back home? I kinda miss her," Venice asked after some time.

"I miss her, too. If she's all better, I don't see why not."

"We should go checkup on her one of these days."

"Okay."

Venice's innocence was what I wanted to protect. Despite all that we've gone through together, the love Venny has for our mother has never deterred. From a distance, I could tell we were getting close to our destination, and I was ready to put my feet up and relax for a little while.

Reaching the shelter, there was a long line, and I couldn't help but groan. I silently prayed that there would be room for us because I was at my wits' end. I don't know what I would do if we had to sleep outdoors tonight. I'm sure we wouldn't survive it.

As we got closer to the door, I crossed my fingers behind my back, just hoping that God would cut us some slack. But of course, God was silent. Before we could reach the entrance, the attendee was beginning to turn people away.

The tears that I was holding back broke free and rolled down my cheeks. Silently, I pulled us out of the line and made my way to the end, where I began to weep. I felt helpless and weary. I wasn't sure how much more of this I could take. I couldn't keep disappointing Venice. This was no way for a child to live.

Sliding down to my butt, I placed my head in my hands. I was grateful that Venice didn't ask any questions and opted to sit down next to me. Resting her head on my trembling shoulder, she wrapped her arms around me, allowing me to be weak.

"Nairobi Xenos." An unfamiliar voice called out, causing me to lift my head.

"Who's asking?" we asked, skeptical.

"My name is Gabriel Hernandez. I was sent in search of you by Raphael. I am sure you know who that is."

Wiping my tears away with haste, I fixed him with the strongest glare I could muster in my state. "Yeah, I know him. What's it to ya?"

"Would you rather y'all sleep outside amid a hurricane and potentially drown to death, or would you like to have shelter and hot food? Your choice."

"Thank God! I pick option two!" Venice exclaimed, standing up, "Especially if that'll help my sister. Ralphie is a nice man. I've met him!"

Gabriel looked between Venice and me before fixing me with a raised eyebrow. "What will it be, Ms. Xenos?"

Put your pride aside, Nairobi. I thought. *Only for a short time. This won't be forever.*

"Fine," I mumbled, allowing him to help me up. "Only because there is a storm coming and there is no room for us here. This is only temporary."

"Yes, ma'am."

I guess He wasn't silent after all.

5

Raphael

We've found her. I re-read the message, anxiety leaving my body. Now I could finally focus on seeing my family with peace of mind. The pit that was in my stomach had settled as I took a sip of chardonnay.

Until we meet again, Nairobi. I mused. *You are probably hating this right now, I bet.*

***

"Kot mennaj ou?"

"Alo Manman," I greeted, brushing past her question.

She was sitting in her favorite rocking chair, arms wide for an embrace. Making my way to her, I brushed my lips against her cheek. I couldn't lie, I was happy to see her.

"How are you, Mommy?" I asked, sitting at her side. "Everything okay?"

"Wi, my son. I wish you'd come to visit more. You know I am getting older." Her Haitian accent weighed heavily on each word.

"Mom, stop it. You know I don't like when you talk like that," I chided, shaking my head at her.

She smiled warmly, her locs shaping her head perfectly, flowing down her back, curling around her hips, and lazily pooling in her lap. "Your father is in his office. Go see him, and afterwards come to the backyard. I've made your favorite."

"Okay, Mommy," I replied, helping her up out of her seat before doing as she asked.

I took my time making my way through the house to my father's study. Like always, the memories played like a movie as I took in our family pictures plastered on the walls. Each picture documented the growth of our small family.

The most distinct change was my Manman's hair. If anyone asked young Ralph what he loved most about his Manman, it was her hair. The hairstyle wasn't widely accepted in the Haitian culture, which made me fall in love with it even more. It made me think about Nairobi and her wicks. She was a bold woman.

34

Continuing down the hall, the pictures just showed the three of us. I was an only child, and honestly, I didn't mind. It was lonely at times, sure, but I always got what I wanted, so I couldn't complain.

Stopping at his door, I knocked twice before entering.

"Papa, I am here," I announced, closing the door behind me.

Taking in its prestige, my childhood came in flashes. I remembered playing in here all the time and getting in trouble for not asking for permission, but it didn't matter to me. I wanted to be just like my father: a well-respected entrepreneur with multiple sources of income.

Looking at where he sat, his glasses lay against his nose as he read the newspaper.

"Alo, son," he peered over his glasses at me before going back to reading. "Ou te pale avek Manman ou?"

"Yes, Papa. Lunch is prepared." I moved to sit at his desk. "No one reads the newspapers anymore."

"Mm. That's y'all problem now. Y'all young folk," he huffed, pushing up his glasses.

I chuckled, slightly. We sat in comfortable silence for a while, like old times. I watched him read, taking in his appearance. He was aging well. Mom was diligent at taking care of her husband, and it was paying him healthily. His once salt-and-pepper 'fro had completely turned white, and his beard and mustache were following suit.

My parents were getting old, and it was time that I took their request seriously. My mom was right.

I rubbed my fingers together, a familiar nervous habit. Being home always gave me the Benjamin Button's.

"Dad," I said quietly. "Don't tell Mom."

And just like that, he was all ears.

"Now, you know I don't keep secrets from my wife." He narrowed his eyes at me. "Kisa ou fè?"

I sniggered at the truth in his words. "I think I met someone."

He leaned back in his chair, taking off his specs. "Ou jwe twòp, ou kon sa?"

"Papa, yon bèl ti fanm, wi. Menm, li pa vle m." I exhaled. "I ain't never felt like this about anyone before. I don't want to make her uncomfortable. What is this feeling?"

He went quiet for a moment, then: "When are you going to bring her home?"

"Soon," I answered. "Her name is Nairobi. Nairobi Xenos."

He let out a deep sigh. "Finally. I prayed that you weren't gay for a long time, and God has answered my prayers. Thank you, Lord."

I rolled my eyes, smirking. "Dad, ou jwe twòp, ou kon sa?"

He laughed. "I won't tell her for now, but you know when it comes to your mother, I can't hold water."

"I know, Dad. I know. I'll let you know."

***

Like always, we had lunch out in the backyard. Mom had the dining table prepared for us with her seasonal China, a little ritual she always did when we were all home together. These were the times that made me wish I had a wife, someone I could love and spoil the way my father doted on my mother.

An image of Nairobi flashed through my mind. She'd make one hell of a wife. Strong and willful, but gentle and compassionate. The way she cared about her sister was more than enough to reassure me that there was more to her than that façade she hid behind.

Just as my father and I stepped out the French doors to the back of the house, the savory smell of rice embraced me causing my mouth to water. I could tell that my father was excited. I watched from the corner of my eye as he rubbed his hands together; giddy. I laughed inwardly, shaking my head. My father was naturally a serious man, but when it came to his wife, he was a totally different person.

"Hungry?!" my mom asked, gracing us with her presence.

My dad immediately flanked to her side, taking the jug of limeade out of her hands, and placing it on the dining table.

"Very," I replied, right on cue as my stomach growled. I rubbed my belly dramatically. "What's on the menu?"

"Diri, pwa nwa, ak legim," she answered, her mother tongue wrapping softly around each word as she moved to sit next to her husband.

Pulling out her chair, she sat down gracefully. It was a rule in our home that no one was allowed to sit until after my mother, as a form of respect because she was the lady of the house. I always thought that my father was doing the most, but it was his way of showing her he loved her.

Watching out for her hair, he moved her tresses to her lap before pushing her seat close to the table. Once she was settled, my father and I took our places at her side. Holding hands, he blessed the food before we ate.

Like every other dinner we spent together, I kept quiet about the illegal work I was tied up in, only sharing the safe details. It felt good to hear laughter and to be home.

At first, I wasn't too keen to be here, but I realized that there was nothing like family. I thanked God for the small victories.

My mind wandered to Robi, again, and I could only imagine what her childhood was like. It was obvious that her life was hard, and I could feel my heartstrings pull at the thought of someone hurting her again. Then there was her little sister, Venice.

Jesus. I thought. *I must protect them.*

"Son?"

I blinked back into reality, "Sorry, yes?"

"Is everything okay?" my mom asked.

"It will be soon. Don't worry, Manman."

She gave me one of her motherly stares, searching my face before accepting my answer. "Okay, baby."

I got you, Robi.

6

Nairobi

Venice and I have been at Raphael's home for a few days, and the owner has yet to make an appearance. I could feel myself getting *too* comfortable here, and that scared me. This place was huge and despite how spacious it was, it was nice and cozy. Venice had made herself at home and planked herself in front of his large flatscreen that was in the den.

Of course, there was a maid who came in regularly to clean up, and Gabriel would also come over to check in on us. It was obvious that he was updating Raphael on how we were doing. Honestly, I couldn't wrap my mind around why this man was being so attentive. He didn't even know us.

"Can you stop pacing?" Venice mumbled, eyes still glued to the screen.

I stopped in my tracks. I felt like I could pull my hair out by the roots. I looked out the window and saw lightning. The trees were beginning to shake from the strong winds. The sun had officially disappeared, leaving the sky a moody gray.

With a groan, I slumped down beside Venice, laying my head in her lap.

"Stop acting crazy, Robi. Everything will be okay." Venice said softly, patting my hair.

Before I could respond, the soft whistle of the house's door system echoed — someone was coming in. I glanced at the clock perched on the fireplace mantel. Too early for Gabriel.

"Hey, Gabe! Venice called out cheerfully. "And yes, before you ask, we ate our fullest."

Venice's innocence allowed her to befriend anyone, and Gabriel was a sucker for her childlike charm. However, I knew better. The energy in the air had shifted and I could tell that the person marching towards our direction was not Gabriel. Raphael was home.

"I'm glad you've been eating well, and that Gabe has been doing a great job of taking care of you guys while I was gone," Raphael's deep, velvety voice resonated through the open space.

"I apologize for leaving y'all alone for this long. I am such a bad host."

"Ralphie!" Venice exclaimed, giggling. "Oh, it's been so long!"

Raphael laughed. "Nice to see you again, Venny."

"Oh no, it's no problem at all. I should apologize for infringing on your space. Thank you for allowing us to stay here. I promise once the storm stops, we will be out of your way." I said, looking everywhere except in those chocolate orbs.

"Ms. Xenos." His voice commanded my attention. "I want you here. Both you and Venice are wanted here. Stay at your leisure."

"So, we don't have to leave?!" Venny asked.

"Nope," Raphael replied. "Stay, Nairobi."

I stared at him, long and hard. My mind was telling me not to trust him, but my body was tired of the struggle and wanted to relax finally. He was trying to give me a way out, but my mind was shifting through all the many ways this arrangement could go wrong.

"I don't know," I mumbled.

Venice groaned beside me. "I'm tired of the outside, Robi. There is a TV here, warm water, and a bed."

Raphael visibly stiffened, fixing me with a glare. I flinched, lowering my eyes.

"…Okay," I whispered, barely audible.

"We can stay."

FIRE AND DESIRE

***

Not long after, I took my leave for the room Venice and I had been lodging in. Venice was still in front of the TV when I left, and Raphael had taken the liberty to whip up some snacks for them to munch on. Sighing, I decided to take a bath.

Stripping down to my undergarments, I glided to the bathroom. I ignored the mirror, not wanting to see the scars that danced across my dark skin.

When I first saw the tub, I fell in love with the bathroom. Memories of my childhood pressed play in my mind as I filled the tub with hot water. Before Mom became an alcoholic, back when Venice was just an infant, Dad was still around. It was a routine for Mom and me to take baths together, but all that changed when one night he just never showed.

Instead of rowing down the conscientious stream of my thoughts, I focused on relaxing in the steamy water. Closing my eyes, I sighed once more, feeling my tense muscles finally begin to unwind.

Maybe we are safe here.

***

Knock. Knock. Knock.

"Nairobi?" A muffled voice called behind the door.

I pried my eyes open, mumbling an answer. I had fallen asleep in the tub and the water had become cold. However, I was too exhausted to care and allowed my eyes to slide shut again.

"I'm coming in," the voice said.

***

I woke up with a start, confused.

Where am I?

Looking around, I realized where I was. Raphael's home. The last thing I remember was being in the bath.

My eyes widened. Raphael was in the bathroom. In the bathroom with me and I was naked.

Throwing the sheets off my body, I squealed at the sight. I was dressed in a silky nightgown.

Feeling violated, I clambered out of the bed and the room.

"Raphael!" I shrieked, scurrying down the hall to the common area. "How could you?!"

Venice and Raphael were at the dining table, eating breakfast. I immediately felt bad for yelling like a mad woman, but who gave this man permission to invade my privacy? I sure didn't.

"Robi, what's wrong? Nightmare?" Venice asked, both confused and concerned.

I shook my head, glaring at the culprit.

How dare he look at my body. Who does this dress even belong to? I rolled my eyes at the thought. *Probably one of his hoes.*

"Would you have rather gotten a cold, or be in a warm bed?" Raphael said smoothly, peering at me and biting into a peach.

"You could have knocked or something! I am more than capable of taking care of myself," I growled, straightening my stance, "I hope this dress is brand-new because putting random clothes on me is crossing the line."

"I did knock, Nairobi. You were barely coherent. I apologize for making you uncomfortable. The water was too cold for you to continue to soak in any longer. I promise to leave you there the next time you fall asleep, if you like." He cocked his perfectly arched eyebrow, taking another bite out of the juicy fruit. "Don't worry, I wouldn't disrespect you like that. I'm sure you met Mrs. DeLuca. I sent her out to pick you up some things to make sure you were comfortable here. I don't mind you bare, though."

I could feel the blood rushing to my face. Catching myself, I moved my eyes from his lips to meet his eyes, and my underarms pooled with sweat. He was already staring at me with a smug look on his face. Those orbs that were normally chocolate were now

45

intensely molten, and it felt like he was peering down into my soul. This man was beautiful, and he knew it.

I sputtered, "Whatever."

"You guys are weird," Venice commented. "Anyway, I was thinking we could go somewhere after the storm. You know how hurricanes do in these parts."

"How am I weird? He's the weird one," I contended, shifting my gaze to my sister. "But yeah, I guess… I don't see why not. Hopefully we can get out of here soon."

"Oh, most definitely! Ralphie can come with us!"

I rolled my eyes. "Raphael will probably be busy, won't you?"

"Aww, really?" Venice asked, putting on her best puppy dog face.

"I'm not weird," Raphael smirked, tossing the peach pit away. "I think I can spare some fun time for you guys. What type of host would I be if I didn't?"

"Yay!" Venice exclaimed, shoveling a piece of pineapple into her mouth.

Annoying.

7

Raphael

I didn't mean to make her feel uncomfortable, but she had been gone for a long while, and I got worried. Venice had mentioned that Nairobi had been gone for over an hour so I went to go check. I knocked on the guest room door and there was no response, so I went inside to see that the space was vacant. The light in the bathroom was dim, so I knew she was in there. Knocking again, I could hear the water sloshing before it got quiet again.

"Nairobi?"

"I'm so tired," she mumbled back. "So tired."

"I'm coming in," I replied, opening the bathroom door.

FIRE AND DESIRE

There she was, asleep in the tub. Snores of exhaustion left her throat as she began to sink deeper into the water. Shaking my head, I grabbed a towel from the rack before pulling her out of the water. Holding her in my arms, I couldn't believe how petite she was. Her body was so fragile, and I was scared that if I wasn't careful, I'd snap her in half. That would soon change because there was no way I would allow her out of my sight ever again.

Despite her chocolatey skin, I could see where bruises were healing up and the old scars. I clenched my jaw, feeling immense anger. If this was Omar's doing, I'd find out soon enough. Pushing the thought out of my mind, I laid her softly on the bed and placed her into a nightgown. I was not expecting to have a woman at my home, but the energy was comforting. She moaned softly, neck resting to the side showcasing her butterflied neck. Running my knuckles against the tattooed column, I resisted the urge to kiss the pulsing vein. She was beautiful.

Tucking her in, I took my leave and made my way back to the living room, where Venny still was sprawled out. I chuckled at the sight. She was also knocked out, slightly hanging off the recliner. Turning off the TV, I picked her up and brought her to where her sister slept. Leaving them to slumber, I left for my office.

Slumping down in the rolling chair, I blew out air from my lungs. I was tired. I still hadn't rested after the drive, and there was work waiting for me. Rustling through invoices that were on my desk, I was interrupted by the office phone ringing.

I let it ring before picking it up. "Pierre."

"I was hoping to catch you earlier in the day, but I got caught up dealing with these hoes. You know how that can get, don't you?" the familiar voice sounded through the speaker.

Annoyed, I sighed. "How can I help you, Mr. Randall? I have more important things to attend to."

"Damn, too busy to chat? Well, I'll go ahead and get to the point," his words slurred, indicating intoxication. "Am I missing something? I thought we were on the same page."

"Spit it out, Mr. Randall," I rolled my eyes. "I don't have time for guessing games."

"You cut me off. Those accounts are frozen."

"I didn't think there would be a need to explain the obvious."

He huffed. "How you just gonna cut me off? I thought the deal was muscle and supply. We ain't finish."

"I don't need you anymore. Simple."

"This how you gonna do me after all these years?" he sneered. "I thought we was brothers."

I laughed. "Brothers? Man, listen, business is business. I don't owe you nothing but a "thank you" for your services, but they are no longer needed."

The line grew quiet before it went dead. Omar had hung up and I couldn't care less. I don't owe him or anyone an explanation. It was obvious that he needed me more than I needed him, and the fact that he even called proved that.

I dialed Gabe's number. He picked up on the first ring. "Yo."

"Omar called me, bitching about my money."

"I was wondering when he was gonna notice. What was he talking about?"

"Jhit said we were 'brothers in crime.'"

Gabe burst out laughing on the other end. I pulled the phone away from my ear, smirking.

"Brothers? He really said that? More like you were breastfeeding him."

"Shut up, Gabe. I'm being serious," I scoffed. "He threw a tantrum before hanging up. Big bad wolf on the loose."

"What do you want to do?" Gabe asked, chuckling.

"Omar is stupid, but not insane. Be prepared for anything, though. People get crazy when it comes to money."

"Shit's 'bout to get real, I see."

"Mhm. I'll hit you up later."

"Ight."

Yeah. Shit's 'bout to get real, indeed. Give it your best shot, nigga.

8

Omar

Who the hell does this boogey-ass nigga think he is? Ain't shit changed since college – still walking around with that superior complex. To this day, I can't believe that he would call 12. There's no forgetting the night that changed my life forever.

I don't take well to people stealing from me, and that nigga had it coming. Ralph always believed he had a halo over his head, and I couldn't stand it. He was bad for business, and I was still looking to get my lick back.

Going to prison can really fuck you up. I wouldn't wish that place on my worst enemies. Luckily for me, I went away on a drug charge. Sammy wasn't so lucky and had to skip town and become a whole different person. His stupid ass did a great job at getting rid of the evidence.

Again, he was fucking shit up. Though, I'm not surprised; I wasn't expecting it to happen so soon. Regardless, he should know better than to mess with my money.

I sneered. Picking up the phone again, I pressed in the numbers, jittery.

"This better be important that you are calling me at this time of night, Mr. Randall. My wife is asleep and if she hears me working, she's going to kill me and I'd have to kill you, too."

"Oh, please," I smirked, putting the phone to my ear. "I'm sure this is more important than your new wife's sleep."

The line went quiet except for the rustling in the background.

"You can talk freely now."

"Raphael Pierre. Ring any bells?"

"Yeah, how could I forget?"

"I need him out of the picture, for good. He's messing with my money."

A low chortle came through the receiver. "Oh really? Funny, you had no problem working with him, even knowing he's a snitch."

I rolled my eyes. "I don't remember asking to be lectured by you of all people. If you had done your job, neither of us would be where we are today. You, hiding in Canada. Me, working under the table. Or should I remind you he's also the reason you had to leave your family behind?"

"There are plenty of people out there who will spend a big penny to break Raphael. If anything, I am doing you a favor by telling you first before everyone else. Don't waste my time."

"What's in it for me?"

"Get rid of him and we'll split everything down the middle," I said flatly. "I'd handle it myself, but... that's why I have you."

There was a long pause.

"Is that a deal, Mr. Xenos? Or should I move along?"

"Deal."

"It's always a pleasure doing business with you." I smirked, leaning back in my chair.

"Wait, before you hang up," Mr. Xenos cut in, "How's Sahara? My daughters?"

"They are all dead, Mr. Xenos. Don't act like you care now. You left them for dead while you went and made another life for yourself," I lied.

"We both know that's not true," Mr. Xenos whispered-yelled.

"No one cares though. So, you have a good night."

Hanging up, I closed my eyes, satisfied. By any means necessary, I'll get what I want.

9

Nairobi

I t's been a week, and the rain had finally slowed down, and I was elated, to say the least. I could tell that Venny was eager to get out of the house, and I would be lying if I said I didn't feel the same. We had been cooped in the house for almost a month, and I was dying to stretch my legs...even if it meant clambering over tree branches.

Being in West Palm, it didn't take much for "our world" to kickstart again, so I was sure that we'd be out of the house in no time. School would be out for another week or two as the roads needed to be cleared, which was good for me, considering I had yet to find a reliable way of getting Venice to and from school. Of course, I could ask Raphael but I'm already living with the man, and I refuse to be viewed as a moocher who can't seem to figure shit out on her own. If anything, asking for help is the reason why both Venice and I are in this predicament in the first place.

Don't get me wrong, I am grateful. If it wasn't for his persistence, we wouldn't have hot food, let alone a place to call our own. Breakfast was prepared every morning, and we never had to worry about someone violating our space. We could just be. What more could I ask for? It was almost too good to be true. Nothing in this world was easy and I hated it with passion.

Letting my mind wander to Raphael, I couldn't help but be disappointed. He was rarely around and despite my comments, I was curious. This man was a mystery and there was a dangerous aura that radiated around him. Those chocolate orbs revealed nothing but held so much depth. Part of me was scared to find out more, but damn, he enticed me. What was he involved in that made him so closed off? He wanted me here and I wanted to know why.

He wanted my trust? Well, he'd have to earn it and today would be the perfect day to try. Since the storm was over, I'd make him remember his promise to Venice. He said so himself, what man would he be if he broke his promise to a child? A man who lacks morals, that's who!

Turning to a munching Venice, her cheeks were full of pancake, like a little chipmunk. There was nothing that could stand in the way of this girl and her pancakes. I laughed.

"I know you noticed that the storm is practically over. Ready to get out of here?"

"Hell yeah!" She exclaimed, gulping down her breakfast, "I thought you'd never ask!"

My eyes widened at her response, choking on my orange juice. "Okay, but watch the language."

"Okay!" Venice replied, smiling. "Do you think Raphael still wants to go out with us?"

"Let's go and ask. I'm sure he won't break his promise."

Taking her hand in mine, I helped her out of the chair. Thanking the maid for her service, we skipped down the hall to where Raphael usually disappeared to for most of the day. Raising my hand to knock on the door, Raphael's voice boomed from the other side.

"...How many times do I have to explain this to you? My patience is wearing thin, and we both know what happens when I lose patience," Raphael growled, abruptly throwing open the door.

My eyebrows nearly touched my hairline as I had never heard Raphael speak above a leveled tone. His nostrils were flared, and his lips were set in a hard line. His brows were furrowed, making the skin between his eyebrows press tightly together. I was surprised to see this side of him. He was furious and it was sexy.

"I'll call you later to make sure the job is done. Do. Not. Disappoint me," Raphael said, hanging up the phone. His face softened the moment he saw us. "What a pleasant surprise. Need anything, ladies?"

"Is everything okay?" I asked, carefully. "Venice and I were coming to let you know that the storm was slowing down, so maybe we could go to the market once everything clears. But, if you're busy, we can just go, just the two of us."

"Please be available," Venice piped up quickly. "My sister is fun and all, but…"

I shoved her, rolling my eyes.

Raphael chuckled. "I don't see why not."

***

The sun was setting, painting the blue sky with a soft red-orange hue. The whooshing of the winds had quieted to nothing but a whisper, and I took the liberty to go snooping. Leaving Venice to watch her favorite TV shows, I wandered down the long hallway leading to the many rooms that filled his home. If I didn't find something to do, I'd lose my mind from boredom.

Taking a random turn in Raphael's mansion-like abode, I came across a room that resembled a man cave. Walking down the steps,

I was amazed at the sight. This space was Raphael's personal game room, and I was surprised. He didn't seem like the type. The walls were covered with all types of games. From board games to video games, this guy was a certified geek. I snickered. I bet he'd die if I told him I found his secret stash of nerd games.

On the other hand, I was impressed. I have never seen anything like it. Scaling the games with my hands, I landed on one of my favorite board games of all time: *Mancala*. I couldn't help the smile that graced my lips. It's been years since I've played the game. It brought back some bittersweet memories, but I refused to allow it to get me down. Putting the box under my arm, I quickly scurried to the living space where Venice sat glued to the TV screen.

I hope she remembers how to play. I thought.

"Venny! Look what I found!" I gushed, holding out the *Mancala* box to her.

"Huh?" she asked, slowly giving me her attention.

"Mancala, girl!" I squealed. "Do you remember how to play?"

Her eyes lit up. "Where did you even find this? Of course, I remember! I always looked forward to beating you on family game nights."

I rolled my eyes. "Please. I let you win, remember? You were such a sore loser."

Venice huffed. "As if! That's exactly what a loser would say... I bet I'd beat you now!"

"Is that a bet?" I teased, egging her on.

"Set it up and stop wasting time," Venice growled, playfully mugging me.

Laughing, I opened the box before placing the wooden board in front of us. Unfolding it, I began setting up the board. I left the choice of game style to Venice so I could play first. We'd play until we were bored of the game. That's how it always was. If we had another player, we'd take turns playing the winner.

Once the game was ready, I took my turn. We took this game seriously, and there was zero talking as we watched each other play for the win.

"Y'all must really love this game, huh?"

I literally jumped out of my skin. We both looked up to see Raphael staring down at us.

When did he even walk in?

I was glad that he wasn't making a scene about my snooping, or that I touched something of his without asking. Still, I opted not to reply and stayed focused on Venice. I would blame the way I was losing on how rusty I was, but Venice was a force to be reckoned with.

Raphael chuckled, settling comfortably on the carpeted floor near us.

"We love Mancala," Venice declared proudly. "As you can see, I am winning."

"Shut up," I mumbled, watching Venice clear the board. "I'm letting you win, remember."

"Sore loser, much?" Venice mocked. "And… I win! Dang, I should have bet money!"

I rolled my eyes. "Whatever, jhit."

"I guess it's my turn now, isn't it," Raphael said, casting me a look before sliding into my spot.

Sighing, I plopped down into the armchair. Believe it or not, I didn't mind losing to my sister. I enjoyed our little banter, and it made the game more exciting.

"Since you lost, how about you fetch us some snacks?" Venice teased, putting on a posh accent.

Spoke too soon, I thought, ignoring Raphael's snickering as I made my way to the kitchen.

Raphael's maid was in her usual spot, moving around the kitchen, and as expected, it smelled delightful. Mrs. Lucille was a quiet Haitian woman, and our conversations never made it past professional. I could tell that she's worked for Raphael for a long time because she never complained, nor did Raphael when it came to her dishes. She still hadn't noticed that I entered the kitchen as she busied herself with meal prepping.

Clearing my throat, I made my presence known. "Hey, Mrs. Lucille. Whatcha cooking?"

Looking up from the pot, she smiled with her eyes. "Oh, alo, Miss. Nairobi. Making some bouyon... dinner will be ready shortly."

Her accent was thick, but it wasn't hard to make out her words. I've lived in the city my entire life, so I was used to it. West Palm Beach was one of the most diverse places on the planet... or maybe I was just biased.

"Bouyon?" On cue, my stomach growled. "I'm starving. But I was sent to grab some snacks."

"Check the cupboard," she said, motioning with her chin. "Whatever you like. And make sure you tell them dinner is almost ready. Di Raphael sa."

"Okay, Mrs. Lucille."

Shuffling through the cupboards, I saw a large bag of dill pickle chips and chocolate chip cookies. Placing the snacks on the island, I knew I wouldn't be satisfied without a glass of wine. With snacks and a bottle of wine in tow, I took a seat next to my competition.

"Is it my turn yet?" I asked, watching Raphael's hands as I set everything down on the glass table. "Mrs. Lucille says dinner is bouyon tonight."

On cue, Raphael's stomach growled.

"Has anyone lost yet?" Venice joked playfully. "Don't worry, I'm almost done annihilating this dude."

Raphael chuckled, casting me a look. I rolled my eyes. *Winning has gone to her head.*

"Bouyon sounds great right about now," Raphael said, eyeing his pot of marbles. But it wouldn't matter if he didn't end up with more on his side of the board.

"Luckily for you, din-din is almost done. Hopefully, these snacks will hold you over," I said, opening the bag of chips before cracking open the bottle of wine.

While Venice played her turn, Raphael took the chance to grab himself a handful of potato chips and sat back to watch his opponent.

I delighted myself in a large gulp of my alcoholic beverage, with a sigh of contentment.

I could tell the game was over as Venny went around the board for the last time. She was going to win.

Moving back to sit next to me, I felt Raphael's eyes burning holes in the side of my head.

He leaned closer. "So, tell me… Nairobi, have you sworn off love?"

"You're so random, you know that?" I muttered, grabbing two cookies from the tin.

I was not in the mood for a game of 21 questions, especially not about my love life.

"Just making conversation."

"Instead of asking me questions, you should really be paying attention. You are about to lose," I rebutted, nibbling on a chocolate treat.

"It's just a game and by the looks of it..." he pointed to Venny whose hand was moving frivolously across the board. "I'm more interested in knowing more about you, woman."

I pursed my lips. *Oh please.*

"I thought we talked about this already. I appreciate all that you've done for Venice and me, but I'm not interested," I said firmly.

I was starting to feel the effects of the wine as it warmed my chest cavity. I was becoming more aware of his presence, and I wasn't sure if I'd be able to keep my thoughts to myself. I just didn't understand what the hype was about. Love doesn't bring anything but trauma and pain. It sure doesn't pay the bills. There are more important things to wrap my mind around than that four-letter word.

"I win!" Venice whooped, throwing her hands up in victory, "Champion tingz. Period!"

Just as I was about to reply, Mrs. Lucille peeked into the living space. "Vin manje!"

"Yay! Food! Right. On. Time," the foodie exclaimed, leaving Ralph and me alone.

"Are you going to answer the question?" Ralph asked, rising to his feet and extending a hand to help me up.

Taking his hand in mine, I raised an eyebrow. "What has love ever done for anyone, Mr. Pierre? Why does it even matter?"

"I agree, loving someone isn't for the weak. Luckily for us, I am strong."

I snorted, dropping his hand. "Mane, whatever."

***

After dinner, I was in need of some fresh air. With the bottle of liquid courage in hand, I exited the front door to the porch. I wasn't surprised to see there wasn't much debris outside the home.

Don't get me wrong, I'm sure there were plenty of areas in Florida that were affected by the storm, but I've been living here my entire life, and outside of Hurricane Katrina, West Palm Beach rarely suffered more than a few tree branches scattered about.

Surveying the area, I was excited to see an egg chair tucked in the corner. Scurrying over to the chair, I made myself comfortable on the damp cushion. I groaned, squeezing the tip of my nose. Raphael's question had ruffled my feathers, and I couldn't get it out of my head.

Being at his house had made me comfortable so much so I wasn't worried about leaving Venice alone. This was probably the safest place we've been since Mom.

Sworn off love?

I topped my glass off, emptying the bottle completely.

Why would he even ask me something so random? If I were to be honest with myself, there's nothing more I want than to be loved, but love has done nothing for me. My parents were AWOL. I wasn't sure how my mother was doing. I didn't even bother letting my mind wander to my father's whereabouts. It hurt too much.

The men that I have encountered throughout my life have done nothing but hurt me. Trusting men is not on my list of prerogatives.

However, Raphael was a different breed of man, but there was something about him that screamed 'stay away'. As tempting as it might be to trust him, I am not willing to bet my life on it. Mentally and emotionally, I was tapped out from all things called love. Honestly, I'm okay with that.

"Hey? You, okay?"

I Looked up from the swirling red liquid in the glass, Venny had poked her head out the door, concerned.

I smiled slightly. "Yeah, just getting some fresh air. You, okay?"

"Yeah, just checking on my sister. You coming back in?"

I nodded my head, shooing her away.

"Okay…" she trailed off. "Well, hurry, I want us to watch this movie before bed."

"Here I come."

10

Samuel

I wasn't a good man. I never put myself on a high pedestal, so when I made the decision to disappear, it wasn't a hard one to make. Looking back, I wish I would have stayed around to protect my family. Before meeting Sahara, I was so deep in the streets that there was no way that I could have let it all go.

Trying to make it in the world wasn't a walk in the park for a Black man. It's easy to tell someone to "suck it up" and "pull yourself up by your bootstraps" when in reality, society was built to keep you on your hands and knees, but I digress.

Going to college was a non-negotiable growing up, and even though I wasn't an idiot, I didn't get into University because of my grades. Football was my savior, it was how I met Omar. He was highly regarded for being connected and at the time, I needed to make a name for myself. My desire to be powerful drove me to many lengths which ultimately had me dealing with people who had the capacity to destroy my world without hesitation.

There weren't many people I was afraid of. The lifestyle I chose to live made it impossible to be a pussy. You were either predator or prey, and no one wanted to be prey.

Back then, I thought hanging out with Omar was a good idea, but I was wrong. From the outside, this man seemed normal but there was something about him that was off.

When I first met him, I was ignorant of how unpredictable and callous he was. We were college kids trying to make ends meet however we could. How could I have noticed?

Nevertheless, I craved acceptance and found it in Omar. Even if that meant getting involved in some crazy shit. I knew that I was way in over my head, but there was no turning back. There's no feeling that can compete with the guilt you feel when you kill someone for the first time. I can still remember watching life leave that man's body. I shivered.

Trailing after Omar began to change me. His greediness had begun to become part of my DNA. I could blame Raphael for my ruined career, but dealing with Omar is what sealed the deal. Before I knew it, I would have to skip town with my tail between my legs, hoping to see another day. I could have been in the NFL, living scotch-free in my penthouse, but here I was, still regretting everything. I would never admit aloud that a part of me was glad Ralph and Gabe were there that night.

When Omar called out of the blue, I knew shit was about to get crazy. "Raphael Pierre," he said. I hadn't heard that name in a while. Of course, his face is all over the news as he was just named one of the richest men in the world. A man of his caliber made you question your own capabilities.

Omar, on the other hand, couldn't stand the fact that small-town Ralph had become a big shot, but, typical Omar, he didn't have the balls to step up to him directly. He never wanted to get his own hands dirty.

As for me, I have nothing against the guy. A job was a job and if money was involved, you can bet your ass I was all in, though I wasn't sure that I would go through with it. Most of all, Omar was not to be trusted, and I had something more important to focus on. For the sake of my mental health, I had to know for sure if my daughters were alive.

Sahara and I had those girls in high school, and the right thing to do was to get married. My parents, God rest their souls, were adamant that I be part of their lives. If they knew how estranged we've become because of my actions, I wouldn't hear the end of it. Still, I had no choice but to leave them behind. It was either me or them.

The only person that I felt I could depend on at the time was Omar… even if he wasn't the best person for the job. Selfish, I know, to rely on someone to give you updates on your own children. What was I afraid of? I don't know. When he said they were dead, I didn't believe it. I had to see for myself.

Going to our old home brought painful memories that I had buried a long time ago. Those memories led me to getting remarried and having more children, but it still didn't make it hurt any less. There was a foreclosure sign in the front yard, but it didn't make the home look any less familiar.

"Sammy, is that you?"

Looking away from the sign, I turned to the voice. "Mrs. Kaitleen?"

"Oh goodness! I was going for my afternoon stroll. I thought that was you! How are you?" Her smile was as kind as I remembered it. "It's been a while since I've seen you around these parts."

The petite woman was in a Nike jogging suit, paired with running shoes to match. I mustered up a smile that probably was painful on the eyes.

"Yes, it's me, Mrs. Kaitleen. I came by to see…" I trailed off, looking at the foreclosure sign again.

"I'm sorry, Sammy," The somberness in her voice caught my attention. "You mustn't have heard."

"Heard what?" I asked, taking a step forward. "What happened here?"

"Maybe you should sit down."

"All due respect, Mrs. Kaitleen, I can handle it. I just need to know where my daughters are."

Sweat had begun to settle between my eyebrows. The Floridian sun was still shining high and bright, and all I could think about was Omar's words. My children weren't dead. It was impossible.

"I haven't seen ya daughters since the hurricane. Y'know that Omar had dealings with ya oldest. Come to think of it, I haven't seen much of him either. The house went up foreclosure way before, though..." Her voice went soft with empathy. "Sahara ain't in the land of the living no more."

I blinked. And blinked again. Sahara's dead.

Memories flooded my mind. I did nothing to protect her or our girls. Tears burned behind my eyes but now wasn't the time to mourn. I needed more information. Though, whatever doubt I had in my mind about my girl's welfare was out the window. The hurricane was just a few nights ago, and if Mrs. Kaitleen said she'd seen them, then I'm sure they are still alive. I just had to find them.

"What did they do with the body?"

"Since there was no one to claim her remains, they cremated the body."

I nearly choked. My first love… cremated. It was almost too much for me to stomach.

This was my fault.

"Was there anything else, Mrs. Kaitleen?"

"Seeing how I've known y'all for a long time and babysat the girls a few times, I have her urn at the house…" she trailed off, pointing to the direction of her home.

"I… uh," I couldn't find the words.

"It's alright, I'll hold on to it until you are ready," she said. "However, you need to find those girls before something bad happens. Their momma's gone to the upper room, I pray. It's your responsibility now to take care of them. They're gonna need their daddy."

"Thank you, Mrs. Kaitleen."

"You be good now, you hear?"

I bid her goodbye before turning back to face my old home.

Fuck.

11

Raphael

Ll good things must come to an end, unfortunately. I can't recall the last time I spent the whole day lazing around. As promised, I went with the girls to the market and ate until my heart was content. Being out acting like a normal human being really takes the stress away. Of course, I had a few people on standby just in case shit got hectic. It would be child's play if I got caught slipping. I wouldn't be able to live with myself if I couldn't protect them.

I was even able to get to know Nairobi better by seeing her in the wild. Those feelings that were pumping through my veins and sending my heart haywire, were getting stronger. Nairobi was a complex woman. Not only was she a great sister, but I could tell she would make a great wife. I watched how she interacted with the farmers and vendors, camping about the rented lot. She was naturally bubbly and caring. That hard exterior she adopted had begun to crumble the longer we shopped. Her smile was like nothing I had ever seen before. Smile lines would grace her face from where they were hidden. Her eyes would sparkle telling her youthfulness. I wanted to see more of it, and I was going to make sure that she'd always smile when she was with me.

Logically, these feelings were dangerous, but there was something about her. I had learned to ignore those ocean-deep emotions ever since I chose this life, but there was no overlooking them when it came to her. A shiver ran down my spine and down to my toes as my mind went back to the conversation we had on the ride back to the house. Venice was doped on homemade sweets and savory meats, so she was knocked out across Nairobi's lap.

"Thank you for coming. Venice had a blast. You made her day." Her words were staccato-like, showcasing that she was distracted.

I was curious to know what had her attention, but I decided to keep our conversation light and casual. From what I've gathered so far about this woman, prying would get me nowhere.

"Only Venice? I was hoping that I was making a good impression on you too," I fidgeted, pretending to be hurt as I took in her profile.

The side of her lip had quirked up before disappearing to a straight line. I felt my heart skip a beat between my lungs. The idea that that small twitch was nearly a smile brought me satisfaction.

"I appreciate the effort, Mr. Pierre. Really, I do."

"Please, call me Ralph, Naye."

I could tell now that I had her full attention. *Naye*? Where did that even come from?

She was peering deeply into my eyes. "That's a first. No one has ever called me Naye before."

I felt slightly embarrassed while having a sense of childish pride. *Naye*. It had a nice ring to it.

"My Naye."

She let out a small laugh. "Let's not get ahead of ourselves here. Ain't nothing wrong with the nickname, but I don't know about the rest."

"Tell me," I pondered. "What is it going to take? I assure you, I am up for the challenge."

"Challenge?" A crinkle formed between her brows. "I am not something to conquer. I am not some board game with made-up rules and points to win. I'm multifaceted and difficult. I promise you, I am not worth the fight."

My eyes narrowed in response, absorbing her truth. Some people would take her honesty for what it was and give up, but I wasn't scared by words. In my world, I had to learn when people were bullshitting me. There was no way she believed that. Right then, I had made up my mind. Nairobi was mine.

"You're right. It's in my nature to master what I want. I have mastered a lot in my lifetime but with you, I want to take my time. I have no desire to conquer you. The mystery is what intrigues me. When you finally give me a chance, I will enjoy every moment of trying to figure you out."

She rolled her eyes.

"Just like those roses, you are delicate, sharp, and perfect. Like a gardener, I will take my time pruning and taking care of you. I will savor every moment of getting to know you, and every time it feels like I've figured you out, I'll be looking forward to the next layer."

Her eyes widened at my confession, and she looked away, flustered, "Uh, um."

"It's okay to love again, Naye." I reached out, toying with one of her locs, "Don't worry. I'll reteach you."

Searching my eyes, her brown orbs melted to hot cocoa. I could tell the walls she had surrounding her heart were beginning to crumble. Wordlessly, I wrapped my large hand around her slender neck and pulled her in for a kiss, slow and cautious, delving into our new experience. My insides had caught aflame, and I wanted nothing more but to sit her on my lap and devour her. She mewled softly, igniting a growl from within me.

"Sir, we have arrived."

Regrettably, our moment was cut short. Nairobi was so in shock that if it wasn't for Venice being asleep in her lap, she would have bolted out of the car. I tried to talk to her before I had to leave but she completely closed me out again. So, here I was, trying to keep my thoughts PG and focus on work.

I blew out a breath, exhausted. Deciding I was just wasting time in front of the computer, I pushed away from the desk. As I began to pack up, the back pocket of my khaki Chicos began to vibrate. Reaching for it, I answered on the third ring.

"Pierre speaking."

"*Poukisa ou pa dem ou te gen yon mennaj?*"

I cursed silently. I should've known better.

"Hi, Manman. I was going to tell you, but it's not official. Yet."

"Sooo, but you tell *papa ou*? I should have been the first to know!"

"Sorry, sorry."

"Well, anyway, *mwen vle ou pote li lakay la.*"

"Manman, I can't do that yet. We are still getting to know each other."

"This is the first time you have said you like a girl. *M vle konnen li. Epi dats it.*"

There was no arguing with my mother once her mind was set on something. I had no choice but to bring Nairobi home with me, and that was extremely unnerving. What was I going to even say to her to get her to take a trip to Miami? I was going to have a serious talk with Pops.

"*Alo*, did you hear me?"

"Yes, Manman. I'll see what I can do."

"You better," she huffed. "Here's Dad."

There was some shuffling sound before I heard my father's voice.

"Son."

"Really."

"Hey, don't get mad at me," he grunted. "You know I can't resist your mother's charm."

I rolled my eyes. *This guy.*

"Yeah, okay."

"When are you coming home with the mysterious lady?"

"If I can get her to come, you mean?"

"You'll find a way, I'm sure."

"It'll be Nairobi and her sister, Venice."

"Nairobi and Venice," Dad pondered. "Authentic."

"Don't start," I muttered, putting my black leather satchel over my shoulder.

There was a muffled commotion over the phone.

"Your mother said there'll be enough food for everyone."

I let out an exasperated sigh. "Great."

"Alright, well, we will talk later. See you."

"Bye, papa."

Sliding the phone in my back pocket, I shook my head. These folks will be the death of me.

***

Among the many hats I wear, being a kingpin has become one of my least favorite, especially since I've met Nairobi and her sister. Before I didn't have to be aware of my day-to-day conversations, but now, I must be cautious with my words. I would hate to implicate anyone.

Getting off the phone with Gabe, I instructed my driver to stay in the area as I wouldn't be long. Shutting the door behind me, I ran my palm down my waves and over my bearded chin. Pulling down the sleeves of my button-down, I sauntered into the office building where all the magic happens. Gabe would be here soon, but I needed to get a head start on collecting money and inventory.

I barely had a chance to open the door before my assistant, Danny Torres, nearly smacked into me. If there was one thing Danny was good at, it was management.

"Mr. Pierre, just the person I was looking for. Hope you are doing well. There is so much I must catch you up on," Torres rambled, scurrying along to keep up with my stride. "Here are those contracts you requested pertaining to your current partners.

Also, I called a meeting with the Jamaicans, and they agreed to our terms."

"Sounds good. Get Mr. Belafonte on the phone so that we can get better acquainted. I'm ready to get the ball rolling," I replied, stopping at the clear doors of my office space.

He nodded, taking his leave.

Stepping into the room, I groaned at the pile of paperwork on the desk. Plopping down in my chair, I began to flip through the documents, resisting the urge to shred it all. As instructed, Torres paged over Belafonte.

"Mr. Belafonte. A pleasure." I said, glancing over spreadsheets of last month's revenue to prepare for any contingencies.

"*Wah gwaan*, Mr. Pierre? Looking forward to making some money with you." His Jamaican accent coated his words, but it wasn't difficult to understand him.

"Same here," I agreed. "You don't mind us working together. I know most of our dealings were through Omar bu…"

"Don't worry about that, mi brotha. Omar like cancer… needed to be cut out."

I chuckled. "I agree. Well, I'm looking forward to our future endeavors."

"Mi too mi brotha. Talk soon." With that, the line went dead.

With a smirk of contentment, I began organizing each file in their respectable places. Moving around the space, I poured myself a shot of Barbancourt and let my eyes wander over to the surveillance cameras, only to see Gabe walking towards the building.

Time for a break.

"Yo, yo, yo! Wassup, playa?" Gabe grinned, carrying two large duffle bags in each hand.

"What took you so long?"

"One word: mi Lucy." He placed each bag on the desk, unzipping both to reveal the contents.

"That's two words, but okay," I rebutted, picking up a roll of hundreds before tossing it back in the bag.

Gabe waved his hand. "Y'know what I mean, *hermano*."

"Well, I got some good news. Belafonte has agreed to partner with us, which means we have the Jamaicans' support. We can officially cut out Omar and deal with them directly."

"Damn, they were quick to get rid of his ass," Gabe said, rubbing his hands together.

I shrugged in response. Not really my problem.

"Welp, let's get this money."

Handing me a kilo of dope, I sliced it open for sampling. Placing a bit on my tongue, I surveyed it for authenticity before nodding my approval to Gabe.

"Say less." Closing each bag, Gabe paged for Torres. "Danny, *las bolsas están listas. Que las chicas corten la droga y cuenten el dinero. Debería haber alrededor de treinta o cuarenta mil dólares. Asegúrate de supervisar esto y documentar cualquier extra. Gracias."*

"*Sí, señor,*" Torres voice came over the intercom. "Oh, Mr. Pierre, you have visitors."

"Who?"

"Mr. Randall, sir. And he's not alone."

Gabe peered over at me, shaking his head.

"Interesting," I mouthed. "Buzz them in. Have the security team on standby for any unforeseen variables."

"Understood. Buzzing them in right now."

"*¿Estás loco?* Now is not the time for unexpected company, especially not Omar."

"Oh, relax. If anyone's crazy, it's Omar for popping up here unannounced."

Gabe shook his head, opening the safe. "*Cristo, me das la presión arterial alta, ¿lo sabes?*"

I stared back at him, confused. "Huh?"

"Nothing, *estupido*," Gabe grumbled, stuffing the duffle bags into the large safe before slamming the door shut.

Fixing his suit jacket, Gabe stood next to me, waiting for Omar and his mystery guest to make an appearance.

"Ah, what a nice surprise," I said. "Samuel Xenos? I wasn't expecting such a reunion."

This was very interesting. Gabe was going to kick my ass, but I was in the mood to stir the pot just a little. I was going to teach Sammy a lesson about being his own person. I wonder if he knew about Omar's dealings with his daughter. Ignoring the pang of guilt, I grinned at how hard Samuel tried to stay expressionless. That would soon change, believe me.

"I thought I should show my face, considering our last conversation was a bit tense," Omar said, making himself cozy in one of my chairs.

"Get comfortable, why don't you," Gabriel muttered, fingers itching to reach into his holster.

"What can I do for you, Mr. Randall?" I asked. "Let's make this quick as you know I am a very busy man."

"I'm giving you one last chance before shit gets hectic. I need my money, Ralph," Omar responds, leaning back into the chair.

"What money, O? We both know everything I work for belongs to me." I cocked my head to the side. "Did you really come down here to stake claim to something that doesn't belong to you? Sounds like desperation to me…"

Omar's jaw ticked. "Ralph, you know how I get down. We can avoid all that if you hold your end. What about our contractual agreement?"

"Don't worry about that. My attorney will get in contact with yours, and they'll work out all the kinks in our agreement."

"I ain't tryna hear that. You owe me. Period."

"Yeah, Ralph. Give the man his money so we can just settle this," Sammy added.

Bullseye. I was waiting for Mr. Cosigner to speak up. It wouldn't be Sammy if he didn't open his big mouth.

"I see you still Omar's lil bitch, Sammy. Same shit, different day," I said snarkily, zeroing in on him.

His jaw clenched, but kept quiet. Yeah, that's what I thought.

"Is that all? I know you ain't come all the way down here to say that. You could've sent that through voicemail," Gabe laughed. "This shit is weak."

"We can either do this the easy way or the hard way, Ralph. Your choice," Omar said, ignoring Gabe.

"I ain't got shit for you, my guy. If that's all, you can see yourself out," I dismissed, waving them away. "Nou met ale."

Wordlessly, Sammy draws out his gun, which resulted in Gabe doing the same.

I chuckled, shaking my head, "How cute. You can shoot, but you won't make it out of here alive, trust me. I don't fear death, sweetheart."

"Listen, it's nothing personal. This can be very simple. Give him his half of the earnings, and we will be on our way," Sammy grounded out.

I looked at the smug dickhead putting a dent in my cushion, and all logic went out the window.

"Y'know Samuel, you make me sick. Dealing with a nigga who doesn't have the balls to handle his own vendettas. Weak niggas flock together," I scoffed. "I wonder how your daughters would feel if they heard that their father is a cold-blooded killer, who killed the only person rocking with them?"

"My daughters?" Samuel's eyes widened. "You don't know shit about my daughters."

Omar looked confused, trying to put two and two together. Gabe kept his position, seeing that my mouth was about to get us in some shit.

"Some father you are... abandoning his children and pointing a gun at their only sense of hope," I laughed, dryly.

Omar giggled. "Nah, don't tell me! Nairobi and Venice?"

Sammy cocked the gun. "Where are my daughters?!"

I grinned, raising an eyebrow, "Safer with me than they've ever been with you, fam. Should I tell them about how you and Omar are like the best of buddies, considering that he's the one selling your daughter for chump change?"

I could feel Gabe's eyes shooting lasers at the side of my head, but I was already on a roll. Sammy looked over at Omar, who shrugged his shoulders. His bitch ass could care less.

"Omar, what is he talking about?"

"Oh please, don't get all fatherly on me," he waved him away. "You weren't worried about them or being a husband to Sahara. That's why you left, right?"

Lowering his gun, I watched tentatively as Samuel contemplated his next move. Giving me one last glance, Samuel stormed out of the office, leaving Omar to clean up his mess. Gabe took the liberty to lower his weapon in response. I raised my eyebrows at Omar, silently asking: What now?

"Nairobi and Venice, huh?" Omar rubbed his goatee. "What a small world. Why am I not surprised... like mother like daughter. That Robi chick got a mouth on her, lemme tell you."

"You keep her name out your mouth, you sick fuck!" I snarled and launched myself at him, but Gabe's arm stopped me in my tracks.

"I'll be seeing you, Ralph." He turned on his heel and left.

"*Hijo de puta*," Gabe murmured. "Good going, Ralphie."

"Shut up."

12

Nairobi

It's been a few days since our little outing, and my mind was still reeling from our kiss. His lips were softer than I imagined and the fact that I could still feel them on mine was beginning to become ridiculous, even Venice was starting to give me the side eye. On the other hand, this caused me to avoid him like a plague, though he's been so busy, I'm sure he hadn't noticed at all. Luckily for me, I also had responsibilities so there was no room to get caught up in my feelings.

Since the aftermath of the storm had come and gone, Venice was gone most of the day, and I had more time to myself than I've had since we left our home.

Staring up at the ceiling in my room, I could tell this man had the dollars. Popcorn ceilings were a telltale sign of lack and by the looks of it, he lacked nothing. I rolled over onto my belly, covering my head with a pillow. Nearly asleep, I almost didn't hear the knock at the door.

"Miss?"

"Yes, Mrs. Lucille?"

"Ralph would like to speak to you, if you aren't busy?"

My eyes shot open, butterflies filling my insides.

"Coming," I squeaked, almost tumbling out of the bed.

Scurrying out the door, I had to slow my pace to keep my excitement at bay. I wasn't even sure where the excitement came from, but needless to say, he had my nose wide open.

When I reached the kitchen, he had his back turned to me, hunched over the island. As I got closer, I could tell that he was eating, and the smell was divine.

"Whatcha eating?" I queried, peering over his shoulder.

"You're pretty quiet. I didn't notice your footsteps," he replied. "Lucille ordered some goat soup for a light lunch. Interested?"

On cue, my stomach growled. Embarrassed, my hand quickly reached for my belly. His laugh was deep from within, making me blush under my skin.

"I'll take that as a yes," he smiled. "Mrs. Lucille, eske ou ka retire yon ti soup pou Naye? Li grangou."

"Pa gen pwoblem."

"Mèsi,"

I smiled awkwardly. "Thanks."

"No problem." He winked. "Come sit. Let's catch up."

I was nervous. God, so nervous. If it wasn't for those damn lips, I would be as cool as a cucumber, but here I was, nearly about to melt. Finally, after some shuffling, I found myself sitting next to him with a bowl of steaming hot soup in front of me.

"How was your day?"

How was my day? My day was filled with thoughts of you, but I would never say that out loud, so I opted with...

"It was straight, for real, for real. I ain't do nothing but just lay in the bed, looking at your non-popcorn ceiling."

Why in the hell would you bring up the ceiling? Stupid.

"Oh, so you noticed that?" His eyes sparkled with amusement.

I groaned inwardly. "Mhm. You are definitely rich."

He laughed. "No, yeah, I'm glad you noticed that I can take care of you."

"Y'know that's not necessary. I can take care of myself, Ralph."

"I don't doubt your ability at all. I would just like to take over, that's all."

I searched his eyes before turning back to my soup. It had cooled down a bit, so I did what any girl would do in this moment, and stuffed my face with dumplings and yams to avoid embarrassment.

"Can I ask you something?" he said, wiping away soup from his lips.

"Sure…"

"What are your thoughts on spending the weekend in the MIA?"

I blinked, unsure. *What was in Miami?*

"I mean… it's Miami. Who wouldn't?"

"What about you, me, and Venice take a mini trip down there to decompress?"

"I don't know. I'd have to think about it," I replied.

It was one thing we were living with him, but another thing to be taking random trips with the guy. I know we kissed and all, but what if it was all a ploy to sell us into a sex trafficking rink or something? People can't be trusted.

"No pressure. I know this is sudden and out of the blue, but please give it some thought," he smiled slightly. "What time does Venice get out of school?"

Looking at the clock above the island, it was nearly time to pick up Venny from school. It would be the perfect time to run Ralph's idea past her, but I was sure I knew her answer already.

"I'm about to leave soon actually," I replied, picking up the bowl to drown the rest of my lunch.

"I would love to join, if you'd have me," he said, picking up my bowl. "We can talk more about Miami…"

90

I nodded, reaching for a paper towel to pat my lips.

"I don't see why not."

***

"Mrs. Bluu brought her dog to class today, and we were able to take turns reading to him," Venice shared enthusiastically.

Ralph had insisted on driving us, which came as a surprise considering he rarely drove anywhere. Being alone with Ralph had my heart running laps, and his scent had me lightheaded. The ride to Venny's school was filled with me trying to keep my eyes forward, but I couldn't help but take in his side profile.

I never thought to be attracted to forearms and biceps, but on Ralph... Christ. They flex beautifully with each turn of the stirring wheel and gear shift. The confidence he wore sent heat pooling in my belly. He was beautiful.

"Nairobi!"

"Huh?" I blinked, looking back to Venice.

"Did you hear me?" Venny huffed. "I asked how was your day?"

"Oh, uh, I'm sorry. My day was pretty chill, honestly. I ain't really do nothing much," I glanced at Ralph, who was side-eyeing me.

"Mm, well, let's go see if Mom is home," Venny requested.

"I don't know if we should pop up there," I hesitated. "We can't drag Ralph–"

"I don't mind, Naye. I would love to meet the person who raised you."

"Well then, it's settled," Venice solidified, hugging her bag to her chest. "I miss her, Naye."

"The nickname is a thing," I muttered rhetorically.

"Yep," Ralph and Venny agreed in unison.

I rolled my eyes, slightly annoyed. I wasn't too keen on going back to that house, but Venny was still a child. Children have the ability to love their parents with no regard for their character. I wasn't a child anymore.

Disassociating, I focused on the soft filler music coming from the radio. I wanted nothing to do with that house. I worked so hard to keep the memories at bay, but now I could feel them itching the surface. I pressed my forehead to the cold glass of the window and worked to regulate my emotions.

Take deep breaths, Nairobi. You are okay. Everything is okay.

"Robi…"

"Naye, we are here."

Blinking into focus, my eyes met a foreclosure sign on our lawn. Memories of a once lively home was replaced with an empty, desolated house with an unkept lawn. I stared at the house, emotions running haywire. I was unsure what to feel but disgust was in the forefront.

Barely registering Venice's words, I watched as movers marched in and out of our old home. I always thought the concept of buying and renting a home was a bit weird. The process reminded me of hand-me-downs at the nearest thrift store. Repurposed for the next person. Gently used.

I was so deep in thought that my brain had to rewind and press play on Venny, who was running across the lawn up to one of the movers. Her hair shook from how fiercely she was speaking. I've never seen this side of her.

Looking away from the scene, Ralph had stepped out of the car, leaving me in the car. I quickly followed, feeling my soul reenter my body.

"Hey! What are you guys doing? This is our home! Where's Mom?!" Venice shouts, pushing against Ralph's arms. "Hey, that goes to my vanity!"

"Ma'am, we are just doing our job," the mover responded. "We aren't allowed to disclose any information in regard to the property."

"We are the owners. I just said this is our home!" Venice had tears streaming down her cheeks. "Tell them, Robi! Tell them this is our home!"

I was too numb to say anything. I could only watch my old life being piled on the lawn where I used to play tag after school. The porch where Venny and I would sit while I braided her hair was no longer ours. This was the same house that carried so much pain. My heart was full. My lips felt wet, licking them, I tasted salt. I hadn't realized that I, too, was also crying.

"Venny, sweetie, I need you to calm down," Ralph urged. "Sir, what will happen to their things?"

"Unless you can arrange for someone to retrieve these items, they will be going to the dump."

Venny screamed, hysterically. I wrapped my arm around my waist, covering my mouth, sobbing. I felt like I was using all my strength to keep from toppling over. We were about to lose everything again, and there was nothing we could do about it. We were helpless once more.

God, why?

"Naye," Ralph looked over at me. "Venny. Your things are safe. I'll have my guys come and retrieve them tonight. Don't worry."

I nodded, hugging myself tighter. Venice whimpered, going lax in Ralph's arms. I turned away from them and wiped my face before walking off the porch. I needed to get away. Where? I wasn't sure, but I was overwhelmed. I had to find mom.

Stopping in front of the car, I pressed my face against the cool window. Clearing my throat, I turned my face to watch the cars that drove past and extras in my story stroll down the sidewalk. Closing my eyes, I relinquished myself to the Florida heat. Ralph needed to hurry up so we could leave. I needed to leave this place and gather my thoughts.

Or search for mom.

"Venny, dear, who is that you're with?" A familiar voice bellowed. "Where's – Nairobi is that you? Where have you guys been?"

Lifting my head from its position, I saw a familiar face in a purple and orange Nike jogging suit.

"Mrs. Kat?" I sniffed and straightened up. "Mrs. Kat."

"Yes, baby, it's me." She came around the car and immediately I fell into her arms.

The embrace reminded me of my mother's. Warm and compassionate. My resolve had crumbled. There was no controlling those ugly tears from pouring out. I think I cried for everything I had been dealing with. From us losing our parents to the stress of having to make ends meet by any means necessary. Seeing Mrs. Kat was the icing on the cake. She reminded me of when my life wasn't shit.

I was lost.

"Hey, hey, it's going to be okay," Mrs. Kat cooed. "Don't let the devil win. Be strong. Keep the faith."

"I don't know if I can, Mrs. Kat. This–," I gestured, "This is too much for me to bear."

"You aren't alone anymore, Naye," Ralph reassures. "I'm here for you and Venny."

I shoved my face deeper into Mrs. Kat's shoulder, embarrassed.

"And your name is?" Mrs. Kat inquired. "I ain't never seen you before."

"My name is Raphael. Raphael Pierre," he replies, reaching his hand out to shake hers. "I plan to remove them from all this."

Leaving the crook of her neck, I looked to Venice, who was quiet, and motioned for her to come to me. She left where she was tucked under Ralph and smushed herself between Mrs. Kat and me.

Shaking his hand, Mrs. Kat said, "I'm Mrs. Kaitleen. So, they've been with you this whole time, I gather?"

He glanced at me. "Yes ma'am."

"Y'all follow me to my home. We have some things we need to discuss."

Silently, we followed Mrs. Kaitleen to her house which was just a few blocks away. As we walked, I could remember taking the same route to her house after school. Our parents were at work, and she would babysit us. I squeezed Venice's hand before wrapping my arm around her shoulder, pulling her closer. I wasn't sure if I could take any more bad news, but I had to be strong.

FIRE AND DESIRE

It wasn't long before we were standing in front of her humble residence. Letting us through the side door, we trailed behind her until we were in the den. The space was just as I remembered. It was my favorite place to be whenever we came over. She was a collector of books. The walls were turned into bookshelves, filled to the brim, and because she had so many, some were neatly stacked across the room. In the middle of the room, sat her oversized armchair, where I'd spend most of my time. Transversely, there was a loveseat, a large moon chair, and a coffee table. Taking our respective places, we waited wearily for the news. For a while, we sat quietly, not sure what we were here for.

"How have you girls been?" She began.

"Surviving," I replied, looking over at Venice, who was still reeling.

She nodded. "I'll be right back."

She got up and left the den. Coming back, she had a tray of butter cookies and a pitcher of what looked to be iced Arnold Palmer, slices of lemon floating inside. She placed the tray on the table and motioned us to take some.

"So, Mrs. Kaitleen, what did you need to tell us?" I asked, pouring drinks for all of us.

One thing about Mrs. Kaitleen, her lemonade and sweet tea were good on their own, but when mixed together... chef's kiss.

"I know life hasn't been easy for y'all. I ain't gonna pretend I didn't know what was going on in that house after y'all's daddy left."

"It wasn't your fault, Mrs. Kat," Venice piped up.

"No, I should've done something, but I was too scared of what that would mean for me and my family. But now that my boys have left the nest, my obligations have changed," she said, leaning over to pat my thigh.

"I spoke to y'all Daddy. He's looking for you two girls," she continued. "He was here a few days ago."

I had nothing to say in that regard. I couldn't care less that he was looking for us. As for Venny, he had abandoned us when she was real young, so I wasn't sure if she remembered him.

"Okay," I said softly. "Have you heard from Mom, then? Maybe we can save the house in some way."

Her facial expression became grim. She paused before getting up and leaving the room. She came back with a vase-like container and placed it on the table between us. It took a second for it to register.

"No way," I whispered.

"I'm so sorry," Mrs. Kaitleen said, softly.

Ralph cursed, running his hand down his face.

"Can someone tell me what's going on? I'm lost. Where's Mom?" Venice questioned, confused.

"Venny, baby," Mrs. Kaitleen said gently, "y'all's momma ain't in the land of the living no more."

"W-what?" Venice stammered, bottom lip shivering. "You mean she's dead?"

"Okay, that's enough," Ralph commanded. "Thank you, Mrs. Kaitleen, but we need to leave. We will be in touch."

Mrs. Kaitleen looked like she wanted to protest but chose the latter.

"Let's go," Ralph instructed, helping me up.

Taking hold of both of our hands, Ralph led us out of the house. The walk back to the car was gloomy and depressing. No one said a word, what was there to say? Today had become a shitshow.

I was grateful for Ralph. There was no way I could handle sitting there after hearing such a thing. Before the alcohol, my mother was my rock. I mustered up the rest of my strength and squeezed his hand. Looking down at me, he pressed a kiss to my hairline.

"We are going to Miami."

"Okay."

13

Raphael

To say I was shocked would be an understatement. I couldn't believe what I was witnessing. The pit that I had in my stomach had worsened. Everything that I had said about Nairobi weighed heavily on my mind as I led the sisters back to the car.

I cursed, silently. I should've just kept my mouth shut. Here I was trying to act like the good guy, but all I ended up doing was using her situation for the benefit of winning an argument. She's gone through so much and I've done nothing but add to her pain.

Such an idiot.

They both chose to sit in the backseat, not wanting to be apart and who could blame them? I don't know how I would react if I learned that my mother had passed away. I wouldn't be able to handle it.

Helping them into the car, I hopped into the driver's seat and whipped out my phone to make the necessary calls to get their things to a safe place. I looked into the rearview mirror to see them holding each other. This shit made me sick to the stomach. Looking between Venice and Naye, I couldn't imagine leaving them behind now that I have gotten to know them. I sucked my teeth with distaste. Samuel had to be a different type of weak to leave his family behind. Mrs. Kaitleen's tone had suggested that there was more to Nairobi and Venice's story than I was aware of. I was sure that not even Samuel knew what happened to them when he left. My hands clenched the stirring wheel.

"Hey, Ralph?" Nairobi's voice was hoarse from emotion.

"Yes, my Naye?" I asked, jaw clenched.

"Are you okay?"

"I should be asking you the same thing," I replied. "How are you?"

Peering into the mirror again, Venice had fallen asleep, and Nairobi was running her hands through her hair. Switching my eyes back to the road, I let my jaw relax, feeling the pain from how hard I was biting down.

"Can I be honest?"

My eyes shot back up at the mirror before looking back at the road.

"Of course, Naye."

"I can't figure out how to feel. I would have never thought that my mother was going to die so soon," She shared. "It's one thing that she's gone, but… there was no one to claim her. She's nothing but dust now."

I stayed quiet, waiting for her to continue.

"Before the alcohol and Dad, she was a totally different person. If anyone needed a textbook definition of what a mother is, she was the perfect example. I don't even know when it got bad, but when it did, I wished that God would just take her away. I was tired of seeing her suffer, y'know?" Her voice cracked. "B-but now, she's gone, and now I'm fucked up over it. I w-wish that God would've given her the chance to change. I wish."

I wasn't sure what to say to her, so I just continued to drive the car until we got back to the house. As soon as I parked, I helped her out of the backseat and pulled her into my arms.

"Just let go," I murmured, tightening my hold. "I gotchu."

I could feel my heart flutter as her body shook against my chest. She fought hard to keep her sobs at bay, but the pain was too much to bear. I held her until her cries turned into sniffles. Tilting her head back, I searched those tear-filled eyes before kissing her. I didn't usually pray, but in that moment, I prayed the sorrow away.

"Ralph–" she began, breaking the kiss.

"Before you say anything, let's get inside," I interrupted, pressing a kiss to her forehead.

She nodded, reaching back in the car to wake Venny. I gently moved her to the side before picking up Venice to carry her inside. Closing the door, I led the way to the front of the house where Mrs. Lucille was waiting for us. Seeing Naye's face, Mrs. Lucille held her hand and steered her towards the living space, while I went to their bedroom and tucked in the sleeping pre-teen.

Taking one more look at her, I shut the door behind me before making my way to where my woman was.

She looked so small, curled up in the lounge chair under a blanket. Mrs. Lucille had sat a tray with her favorite tea set and some Haitian bread on the coffee table. As she poured us each a glass, the smell of ginger filled the room, calming my nerves. She handed Nairobi a large white pill, which she accepted with a small smile, before taking her leave.

Dunking a piece of bread into the tea, I blew on it before taking a bite. I closed my eyes, my childhood blooming in my mind. Opening my eyes, I watched Nairobi do the same. It made me happy that she was cultured.

"My Naye?"

"Mm?"

"What were you going to say before I interrupted you?"

She downed the last of her tea, setting the delicate cup back on the tray.

"Ralph, I don't think this is a good idea. You and I, I mean."

"Why?"

"We are worlds apart. My life is a shitshow, Ralph. Plus, I already told you I don't need a savior."

"What if I told you that I love you," I asked, peering over my glass.

"I would call bullshit and tell you not to piss me off," she retorted. "That's not a word you just throw around."

"That's the thing. I'm telling the truth, but don't worry… in due time, you'll accept the truth," I countered, setting my cup on the tray as well.

"You're so arrogant!" she growled, standing up.

"Okay, yeah, no, my intentions aren't to make you upset," I retreated, seeing how visibly upset she was.

Her eyebrows were furrowed, and her top lip curled up. Her mind was troubled, and I wasn't helping. I wasn't trying to stress her even more.

Getting to my feet, I made my way to her, gently pushing her back down into the chair and taking her hands into mine.

"Listen to me. I am not trying to add to your stress, matter of fact, I want to elevate all of it. I know that love is a scary thing for you and today didn't help either, but I am telling you the truth," I reassured. "Rest assured, I am sure about my feelings for you. I will protect you and your sister. The moment we met, I couldn't stop thinking about you. I even told my parents about you… which is why we are going to Miami."

"What!" she gasped. "Your parents?"

"Yes, and I know it's too soon, but my mother insists," I explained. "If it makes you feel any better, you are the first woman to ever step foot in my childhood home… to ever meet my parents. I have no intention of letting you go now that I have you here with me."

"Ralph, I'm not who you think I am," She said, weakly. "I'm tainted in the worst way. If you knew the truth…"

"My heart doesn't care. It doesn't matter. I want you and everything that comes with you," I insisted. "Let me in."

"But the parents though?" She whispered-yelled. "I'm not ready!"

"I know, but we've been summoned. You know how that goes with foreign parents."

She sighed, "Oh, Ralph."

I kissed her forehead, nose, and lips. As much as she resisted, her body slowly relaxed against her will.

"It's going to be okay," I smiled brightly. "You'll see."

She laughed breathlessly, "Sure."

"Beautiful."

FIRE AND DESIRE

***

As promised, we were being chauffeured down I-95 to see my parents. Venice hadn't said much or eaten since learning the news about her mom, and I could tell that it was beginning to affect Nairobi. I was hoping this trip would help both of them. Sometimes getting away can help heal the spirit, and we definitely needed it.

"Okay," I clapped my hands together. "I know we're only here for three days, but I'm sure we can get into some trouble while we're here. What do you think, Venny? We can go down to Wynwood Walls, look at art, eat some Haitian patties…?"

She hummed, keeping her eyes on the passing cars outside her window.

"I'm definitely down. It's been years since we've been down south. I'm looking forward to getting some pictures and good eating." Nairobi chimed in, "I'm getting hungry just thinking about the diri ak legume. Oo wee."

I chuckled, feeling my phone buzz.

Make sure you bring them to the house. I cooked. The text read.

We had enough time to waste before I would have to steal Nairobi for the rest of the night. I was nervous, but for her, I'd do anything. Reaching into the side of the door, I handed Nairobi a small-sized bottle of La Marca and a glass flute. I could feel Venny side-eyeing me, which made me send a wink her way before handing her a chilled Sprite.

"Luckily for you, my mother is a great cook, and she insists we have lunch at the house," I said, sliding the device back into my back pocket.

"Can I just say it's crazy that your mom wants to meet me," Naye commented.

"I don't think it's crazy at all. In fact, I've been waiting for the right time to ask both of you to come meet my parents, so this is perfect and right on time if you ask me," I refuted.

"But I'm not the type of girl you should bring home to meet the parents," she sighed, staring down at her hands.

"I know what I want, Naye, and that's you. Nothing can change my mind... not even you," I responded, pressing my lips to her cheek. "Don't worry, I gotchu."

She gave me an intense look before turning her attention to Venice, whose face was buried in the window.

***

"That was so much fun!" Venice exclaimed. "We definitely have to print those pictures."

It was nice to hear Venice's voice and her sister's laugh. I sighed in relief.

Thank goodness.

"I'm glad," I responded, wrapping my arms around Naye's shoulders.

She relaxed into my arms, her shoulders dropping with relief. I could tell that hearing her sister's voice had calmed her nervous system. Checking my watch, it was nearly time for lunch at the Pierres' residence, and they would be expecting us soon.

"Y'all hungry yet?"

On cue, their stomachs growled, causing them to wrap their arms around their bellies. The sisters smiled awkwardly, making me laugh.

"Alright, let's get going," I said. "I do have to warn you though… my mom probably makes the best food in the world."

"Oh, I'll be the judge of that. For sure," Venice winked, leading the way back to the car.

The drive to the house was like night and day compared to the drive to Wynwood. Venny had lightened back up to her normal self, which eased the tension in my chest. She was currently teasing Naye about her inability to whistle. To Naye, she would rather have her sister make her the butt of the joke than to never see her smile again.

"Okay!" I exclaimed as we pulled into the long driveway.

Parked in front of the car garage, we all waited until the driver opened the door for us before exiting the vehicle. Before we could approach the door, my parents were already making their way to us. Bidding the driver a farewell, I led the jittery women to meet the old folks.

"Oh goodness, Cherie. Tifi yo bèl, wi, Ralphie," Mom gushed. "Gade kijan yo bèl. Antre, antre pitit mwen."

"Nairobi, Venice," I introduced. "These are my parents, Fils Pierre and Roselin Pierre. Father and mother, this is Nairobi and Venice Xenos."

Nairobi reached out her hand to shake my mother's hand but was pulled into a hug, then repeated the same with Venny. Peering over at my dad, he gave a small nod of approval. I immediately felt a sense of pride wash over me. I had done good.

The ladies quietly allowed my mother to lead them into my childhood home. I didn't bother trying to intervene because I was sure they were safe in her care. Plus, my mom would have kicked me out of the kitchen if I had followed, so I took a mini detour to my father's office.

"So, that's the girl you've been hiding from us?" Dad said as soon as we both sat down. "She's a beautiful addition to the family. She's Spanish."

"Thank you, Dad," I hummed. "And yes, she's mixed. Black and Dominican."

"Mm, what's their story?"

"It's a long one for another time," I dodged. "But let's just say they needed someone to be at their side, and I became that for them."

"Do you plan on making her your wife?"

"Isn't it too soon to be thinking about that?"

"Oh! Ou te dem mwen li te menaj ou?"

"I just don't want to scare her away. She's been through a lot already."

"Which is why you should make her your wife."

I knew he was right, but if only he knew what it would require making her my wife. There was so much on the line, and I was barely scratching the surface. The idea of making her my wife wasn't the problem, but I would have to give up everything I built to make sure she and our family were safe. And I wasn't sure I was ready for such a big change. Now would be the perfect time to ask for advice, but neither of my parents knew how deep I was in this drug shit, and if they were to ever find out, they would be devastated.

"Well, son, you know I've always made it a point to raise you to be a righteous man. Don't disappoint yourself by making the wrong decision. You don't want to lose a priceless treasure, trust me."

"I hear you."

"Other than that, you okay?"

"Yeah, I'm okay. It's been a lot going on these past couple of days, but nothing I can't handle."

My father opened his mouth but was interrupted by a knock at the door.

"Manje a pare," Mom said through the wood before pitter-pattering away.

"That's our cue."

Making our way to the dining area, both Naye and Venny were helping my mother set the table. Usually, we'd sit outside in the back to eat dinner, but since we had outside guests, Mom felt it was necessary to eat inside. I watched silently. Dad was right. There was no way I was letting anyone else take my place. Nairobi would be my wife.

Like always, us men pulled out the chairs for the women and waited until they were comfortable before taking our seats. The table was plated with my favorite. Since it was lunch, there were Haitian patties, fritay, and to wash it all down was homemade passion fruit juice. My mouth began to water as I reached over to hold my father's hand while he blessed the food.

"Amen," we said together before piling food onto our plates.

I adjusted my tie, awaiting the prying.

"Can I just say, it's so nice to finally meet you both," Mother began. "Ralphie has always been a bit... how do you say 'chich' in English?"

I closed my eyes to stop myself from rolling them.

"Stingy," Dad replied, chuckling.

"Oh yes, stingy! Yes, Ralphie has always been chich when it comes to certain things. I don't know where he got that gremas from."

Nairobi smiled, her eyes twinkling as she caught my eyes.

"It's nice meeting you as well," Venny piped up. "Ralphie was right, you are a great cook."

Naye laughed. "I agree."

I could see my mom's head grow large from the compliment.

"Well, since you both are my daughters, Ralphie has to bring you to come cook with me," she said, eyes sharp. "For a long time, I was worried, y'know? Ralph never brings home women. All work, no pleasure."

I shoved a piece of griot into my mouth, turning to my dad with pleading eyes.

"Cherie doudou, our son does have to work."

"Ebyen…"

"We would love to come… when Ralph has time, of course," Naye spoke slowly, tucking a loc behind her ear.

It was Father's turn to look at me with raised brows.

Swallowing a bite of plantain with pikliz, I nodded. "It'll be no problem."

"How long are you guys going to be down here?" Dad asked. "Your Tonton is in town, by the way."

Mom immediately rolled her eyes. "Baby, really? He just got here…"

I smirked. One thing about my mother, she was easily annoyed and her brother, to her, was a big-time nuisance, but in a big-brother type of way. He was a big partier and was good for throwing the best Haitian parties in all of South Beach. Him being in town meant the obvious... there would definitely be a party tonight and since I was here, there was no missing it.

"Gotta love Tonton Franz."

"Wouldn't you rather spend time with your Mommy?"

That was a trick question. Of course, I wanted to spend time with her, but also, I wanted to spend time with my uncle, and it would be the perfect opportunity to take Nairobi out on the town. I was sure she would enjoy a bit of late-night fun.

"Yes, Manman, but wouldn't you rather me spend time with your future daughter-in-law?"

Naye, who was sipping on her juice nearly choked, spittle running down her chin. I winked, enjoying the balance of soft and crispy patty I was scarfing down. There was nothing I enjoyed more than food. To me, food meant culture.

Upon hearing my response, a big smile graced my mother's face. I could hear my father sigh contentedly at the sight. This guy was head over heels for this woman, it was almost sickening. I hoped for the same with Naye.

"Daughter-in-law?" Naye mouthed, using a napkin to clean her face.

"I knew it!" Venny bellowed. "I knew it. Nairobi you have to say yes, or we will never have Mrs. Pierre's cooking."

"Oh, pitit mwen, rele m Rose, and you can come eat anytime," Mom said pointing to her husband. "Call him Fils."

"Great!" Venny laughed, biting down on a plantain. "I can get to this."

"Venny, your manners!" Naye gasped, still reeling from my earlier comment.

"Don't worry about that, my daughter. This is your home now," Mom gushed. "I always wanted a daughter, but after having Ralphie... he was more than enough."

"Then it's settled. There is plenty of space for a weekend stay," Dad added.

"Are you sure? We just met... I don't want to impose," Naye muttered, nervously.

"Yes, pitit mwen, we are sure," Mother replied. "You go have fun with my Ralphie. Venice and I will do what girls do. Maybe bake cookies and catch a film? What do you think, Venice?"

"I'm down. Go Robi. You need it," Venny smiled, but her eyes showed how much she'd matured. "Brother-in-law?"

I hummed. She turned her gaze onto me. It was rare for Venice to take anything seriously, but I could tell she had something to get off of her chest.

"Protect my sister, okay?"

I could barely register my mother's awing in the background as I absorbed her words.

"You have my word, Venice."

***

After lunch, I stepped away to make a few stops around town to get ready for tonight. I wanted to make our date fun and laid-back. Venny was right, Naye needed a break, and going dancing would be a perfect way for her to let her hair down. I had left them under the impression that I had some personal business affairs to attend to, but really, I wanted to get something special for Naye to show her I was serious. My mother was so excited to have some time with them that she practically threw me out of the house.

Signaling my driver to pull to a stop at the Aventura Mall, I told him to take a break while I shopped. Checking in with Gabe and Danny, they updated me on everything boring concerning the company — the whereabouts of both Omar and Samuel, and any distribution issues. According to Danny, everything was going as planned. The Jamaicans were working diligently at keeping their end of the agreement. Product was moving faster now that we'd cut out the middleman, which made sense, considering he was like your everyday crackhead. Gabe was also doing his part by keeping an eye on both Omar and Samuel, because to hell with niggas popping up unannounced around my shit ever again.

Killing time, I picked out a few items that I would love to see Naye wear. Stopping in a jewelry store, I knew it wouldn't be right to leave Venice out, so I had one of the retailers bag up a bracelet with a few charms. Checking my watch, I rang up my driver to come and scoop me up. If there was one thing about Franz's parties, there was no doubt it would be jumping. Still, I wanted to be fashionably late.

With bags in tow, I moved to the exit, hyperaware of my surroundings. Just as the car rolled around, my phone rang.

No Caller ID.

I rolled my eyes.

"Pierre speaking."

"You petty muthafuka."

I smiled. "How may I help you, Samuel?"

"My daughters' nigga!?"

"Listen, man, this is funny," I chuckled. "When I put two and two together, I felt like the angels were singing from above."

"You know I'm gonna kill you, right?"

"Nairobi would hate that, but you can try."

"What do you want, Raphael."

The way he spat my name, I could tell I hit a nerve.

"Samuel, let's keep it a stack. I ain't the one to hit below the belt. Y'know, Sammy, you still the same wetneck nigga that still tryna be somebody's errand boy." I sneered, hopping in the back seat. "When you gonna man up? You really think I would hurt those girls? You are fucking delulu, like dem kids say nowadays."

I entered the car. "You always loved hanging out with that snake and look at you now…"

"You don't know shit."

"Tsk, please. Tell that bitch Omar I said hello."

"I want to talk to my daughters."

"Gyet Manman," I growled. "They. Ain't. Hostages. Call them yourself."

I ended the call, shaking my head. The audacity of this nigga… to call and try to check me. Me? I am Raphael fucking Pierre. I answer to no one.

14

Samuel

ello?

HThe familiar voice spoke over the speaker. Her voice reminded me of the past. Raphael was right, as much as I hated to admit it. Yes, we were sinners, but Raphael wasn't the type to sell his soul. Still, letting my daughters keep dealing with him would compromise their safety in the end. It would be a long shot, but I had to try to fix our relationship somehow and this was the first step.

"It's me," I croaked, my throat dry from the lack of moisture.

I decided to call her. It's been years since I heard her voice, and it made my heart squeeze.

"Dad?"

"Hey, baby," I answered softly. "How've you been?"

The line went quiet.

"What do you want?" she asked slowly.

I let out a dry chuckle. "Can't I just check up on you? See how my oldest is doing?"

"Don't patronize me, Samuel."

Ouch. I deserved that.

"How's Venice?" I tried again, popping a squat on the toilet.

"You know, it's really hitting me that my life is just a damn game to you," she sneered. "I know she's dead, Dad. You didn't have to make an exception, trust me."

"I understand that you are upset with me," I said quietly. "I'm sorry."

"Is that all? Because I'm hanging up."

"Nairobi, wait." I pleaded, bent over my knees, elbows digging into the tops of my thighs. "You need to listen to me. Raphael is not who you think he is."

"Nah, I don't need this from you," her voice jumped an octave. "You don't get to call me and give me a directive."

"You don't even care to ask me how I even know that name?"

"I could care less!" she shouted. "I may not know much about the man, but I know you, and you are the last person on Earth that I would trust. Save your minutes and don't call me ever again."

"Wait!" I begged, only to hear the dial tone.

"Fuck!" I hissed.

*****

"I was wondering when you were going to call," he said. "Honestly, it's nothing personal."

"I should have known not to trust you," I sneered.

"But somehow you always find yourself dealing the same cards." Omar chuckled dryly. "Sounds like Stockholm Syndrome to me, but what do I know? I'm just your everyday pimp."

"Mane, whatever," I clenched my jaw, temples pulsing. "What are we going to do about Raphael?"

He guffawed, "Now we're talking! Here's what we are going to do."

I knew I was going to regret this, but there was no turning back now. There was no way I was going to allow my daughters to spend another second with that man. If anyone was going to take care of them, it would be their father. Period.

15

Nairobi

Taking a deep breath, I stood in front of the vanity mirror, wearing the dress that Ralph brought me while also trying to shake the nerves away. I tried to keep my mind off my father, but the feeling of uneasiness continued to fill my belly. Hearing from my father was the epitome of a bad omen, especially after finding out my mother was dead.

"Shake it off, Naye," I whispered to the pretty face in the mirror. "Focus on having fun. That's it."

Naye. There goes that nickname again.

Knock. Knock. Knock.

"Come in," I called, rubbing my sweaty hands through my locs.

"Damn, sis!" Venny exclaimed. "Looking good!"

"Language, jhit!" I lightly scolded. "You think so?"

I had to squeeze all of my curves into a fitted strapless brown bodycon dress. I wasn't much of a heel type of girl, considering I was always on the run from something, but these brown French-style heels were perfect. Honestly, I was impressed.

"You look very pretty," Venice smiled, "You need to relax and have fun, sis. Ralphie is a good guy."

I groaned, looking back into the mirror.

"Ugh, I know. It's just… this is my first time really going on a date with a guy," I muttered. "The only guys I ever had encounters with paid me for my services. Ralphie, well, he's different, and I don't know how to act."

"Be yourself. He loves that," Venice said, winking dramatically.

"When did you get so mature?" I asked, laughing.

She shrugged. "What can I say? You've rubbed off on me, sis."

"I'm so proud of you, y'know that, right?" I blurted.

"Of course! What's not to be proud of?" she gloated. "It's me we're talking about."

I laughed.

"Well, I guess you're right. What's not to love?" I said. "I'm glad God chose us to be sisters. I wouldn't want it any other way."

"Oh, stop, you're going to make me cry," Venny groaned. "You just need to get out of your head and have fun."

"You're right," I muttered, looking at myself in the mirror again. "Have fun… what's that again?"

As Venny was about to reply, a firm knock scraped against the bedroom door.

"Naye," that deep, masculine voice called behind the door. "The car is ready for us out front. No rush… just letting you know that I'll be waiting for you downstairs."

"Eeek!" I whispered, half-squealing. "That's Ralph."

"Who else would it be?" Venice whispered back. "Well, say something, dummy!"

"Uh, um, yeah, okay!"

Venny facepalmed herself.

"I'll be down in just a second."

He laughed. "Take your time."

Soon after, I heard him patter away from the door, and I let out a long breath. *Whew.*

***

I couldn't believe I was about to be alone with the male species... especially with someone who genuinely wanted my attention. Usually, I was getting paid for my services, but with Raphael, all I had to do was show up. He was a gentleman, through and through.

On our way to our destination, he refused to give me any hints about what we were doing — only that "I needed to let my hair down for once." Corny, but I let him lead. It wasn't long before we approached Miami Beach. I couldn't help but feel excited. It was the weekend, so a swarm of people was expected.

Parallel parking near the beach, Raphael leaned over into my space, eyes searching for God knows what. Unable to hold his stare, I looked away.

"What?" I asked. "You're staring..."

"I know. I'm just reminiscing about the day I first met you. You were cold, but I knew it was just a façade. And now look at us... about to go on our first date," he said. "How does that make you feel?"

"Well..." I was unsure how to answer without sounding emotionally damaged — which, in fact, I was.

"You can be honest,"

"I've never had a guy show real interest in me besides, of course, wanting to bed me," I said, looking past him. "I was skeptical at first when you started courting me, but now, I feel like I can trust you... to a certain degree, I mean."

"I'm happy to hear that you trust me," he smiled. "I just want you to focus on having fun tonight. I will watch over you. No harm will come to you when you are with me. Okay?"

I nodded, still unsure of myself.

"You ready, cheri?"

"Yes."

***

Meeting Tonton Franz was… interesting. Ralph made sure to introduce me as his girlfriend because Franz was ready to make his move on me. I nearly choked on my wine.

Franz was your everyday party type of guy, and he wore it well. He was just as handsome as Ralph but aged like fine wine. I could tell that he had all the ladies back in his day.

The night was spent dancing the night away and throwing back shots of rum. When it was time to leave, I could barely walk straight. Raphael didn't waste time when it came to having fun and breaking bread. I couldn't even remember the last time I got this shit-faced. I felt my mind wander, but I shook away the past memories. I didn't feel like dwelling tonight. Tonight was about me enjoying myself, and that's exactly what I was going to do.

Ralph gave up on me walking and carried me back to the car.

"Ralphie," I muttered, leaning my head on his shoulder. "Why me?"

"Why not you?"

"You know nothing about me," I replied, holding onto him tighter. "From what you've learned so far, I know you know that my life is in shambles. My mom is dead. My father is a walking catastrophe who cannot be trusted. What does that make me?"

"You're right. There is a lot about you that I don't know, but I'm here. Everyone has skeletons in their closets… it's called life. I wanna be with you because of who you are. Independent, compassionate, loving, funny… the list goes on." He gave me a squeeze. "I'm glad I met you because you make me feel something. For a long time, I thought that all I needed was the bag, but you made me see the world in a different light. It's scary, but I think I want this with you."

I was speechless. *This man.*

"I don't know what to say," I hiccuped. "Whoops, my bad. I ruined the moment."

"No, you didn't," he smiled. "It's a lot, I know, but it's the truth. And here we are."

Placing me on my feet, he helped me into the car, making sure I was strapped safely before closing the car door. I couldn't help but feel safe. It smelled of woodsy, fresh cologne, Irish Springs soap, and 100% man. I snuggled deeper into the leather seats, making myself comfortable.

"Ready?" he asked once he got in. "I wanna show you something… if you don't mind?"

I nodded, not wanting this night to end. *Take me anywhere.*

Maneuvering out of the parking space, he drove us into the night. For a while, we rode in comfortable silence, windows down. Taking in a deep breath, the salty air was therapeutic. The stars were out, shining extra bright tonight. It was almost too perfect.

Suddenly, the car rolled to a crawl before coming to a halt.

"We're here," he said, turning off the ignition.

Blinking away the intoxication, I still couldn't register where I was. We were parked in an alley between two buildings. Now, I wasn't so sure what to expect, so naturally, I was starting to worry.

"Uh, where are we?"

He snickered, stepping out of the car. "Don't be afraid. Trust me."

Coming around to my side, he helped me out of the car. Holding me close, he led us to the side of the building. Giving a wink for reassurance, he knocked on the door. Not long after, a man wearing a bellhop uniform let us in.

"Hola, boss. Buenas noche, señorita," the man greeted, flashing a dazzling smile that could charm any woman. Luckily, I was already spoken for, so I just gave a small smile in return.

"Hola, Enrique. This is my girlfriend, Nairobi Xenos," Raphael introduced us. I gave a small wave.

"Could you lead us to the art gallery? There are some pieces I would like for us to look at..."

Wide-eyed, I looked up at him, only to see him already staring down at me. I felt my blood rush to my face. I was having a hard time hiding my smile.

"Si, Señor, right this way."

We followed Enrique through the hotel, the place was still buzzing with life.

"Once we get to the elevators, you will press PH for the rooftop. That is where you'll find the gallery," Enrique directed, his accent coating every word that left his mouth.

Leading us to the elevator, Enrique bid us farewell as he went to help the other patrons. Holding me near, we rode the elevator all the way to the top. Coming to a stop, the door slid open— immediately, the smell of acrylic paint and tropical air freshener filled my nostrils. In awe, I slipped from Ralph's arms into the cool air. We weren't the only people wandering around, taking in the paintings.

"Champagne?"

Turning to the voice, the server had wine flutes aligned on a golden platter. Taking two, I thanked you.

"You fit right in with the rich folks," Ralph commented as I passed him a glass.

"Thank you," I responded. "I can't believe they have these types of experiences in hotels. That's pretty dope, honestly."

"I think so, too, which is why I bought the space."

I turned to Ralph so quickly, I nearly gave myself whiplash.

"You own this place?" I gawked. "Why am I not surprised?"

He laughed. "I own a few hotel chains up and down the coastline."

I shook my head, smiling. "This is crazy."

"Take a look around. See if any of these pieces speak to you," he said, giving me a little nudge.

I took a deep breath and let my feet carry me wherever, until I stopped in front of a painting of a black woman draped in the Haitian flag. She looked beautiful, strong, and courageous. She represented everything I wanted to emulate: feminine prowess.

"This one," I whispered, subconsciously reaching to touch the artistry.

"Ah, Madam Toussaint," Ralph said behind me. "Famous painting from the Civil War era. She cost me a fortune. Many people come here at the beginning of each year, hoping that I would sell them the painting, but I could never part ways with it."

Looking back at him briefly, then turning back to the painting, I sighed. "She's beautiful." I took a sip from the glass. Whoever the artist was, they deserved all their flowers.

"She's yours."

I nearly spilled the alcohol.

"What do you mean?" I gasped, coughing slightly, giving him my undivided attention. "I can't afford to buy this... as beautiful as she is."

"Listen, when you are with me, there's nothing you'll ever want that you won't have." He wrapped his arms around my waist. "Trust me."

I began to chew on my bottom lip. *Was this normal? This can't be normal.* Before I could get deeper into my thoughts, the voices in my mind were silenced by soft lips. I gasped, opening my mouth to receive him. Our tongues danced together at an even pace as we got to know each other. My belly pooled with excitement, and I could feel that I intrigued him as well.

I moaned softly. *My, my.* I wanted him. Badly.

"Please accept the painting as a thank you for spending the night with me," he said, breaking the kiss.

"Okay, but only if you accept my payment of gratitude," I whispered, looking up at him through my lashes.

"Naye, we don't—"

"I want to." I wrapped my arms around his neck. "Please don't reject me. I need this."

"Okay," he said, taking my empty glass out of my hand and placing it on a tray of the nearest server. "Sir, I want that painting taken off display and wrapped for delivery."

"Yes, sir."

"C'mon." Taking my hand, he led us back the way we came. "We can stay here for the night."

I giggled, letting this beautiful man drag us through the gallery like teenagers in heat.

16

Raphael

She was beautiful. Naked and at peace. I didn't want to wake her, but we had to get back to reality— whatever that might be. I ran my fingers down her arm, skin soft like butter. She smelled of shea butter, coconut oil, and me. I planted a kiss on her shoulder before taking my leave to the bathroom, where I took my time to wash up.

I smiled. It was hard not to reminisce on the night before. Unfortunately, all good things must come to an end. As much as I'd like to stay here, it was time to face reality. Feeling refreshed, I wrapped the towel around my waist and left the bathroom. Room service was always on time and good about making themselves scarce. Piling a plate high of breakfast foods, I poured some OJ into a tall glass before going into the room, where my girl lay asleep. Placing the goods on the bedside table, I gently ran my finger down the length of her face, causing her to stir under my touch.

"My Naye," I said, softly. "It's time to wake up."

She moaned, drowsy.

"Five more minutes, Ralphie."

Ralphie. That's new.

"I got you breakfast."

And just like that, Naye opened her eyes, ready to dig in. Handing her the cup of OJ, she kept her eyes on the glass, avoiding eye contact. Cupping her chin with my hand, I lifted her head to meet her gaze.

"You never have to hide from me," I muttered, pressing my lips to hers. "You're mine and I am yours."

A beautiful smile graced her face that made my heart race and blood rush to my lower region. I groaned. *Gahdamn.*

"You need some help with that?" she asked, softly.

Her eyes twinkled with so much emotion I was drowning in them. There was no way I was going to allow anything or anyone to stand in the way of our love. I've never felt like this for anyone, and it scared me, but I still wanted to explore where this encounter would take us.

Searching her eyes for confirmation, I smirked. "Very much so."

***

The drive back to my parent's house went without a hitch, however, my overdramatic mother didn't want us to leave, so I had no choice but to promise we'd be back to visit. I could still see my dad giving me the side-eye as I reassured her that I would do a better job of visiting home. I was sure he was going to make sure I was a man of my word.

"So that's how parents are supposed to treat their children," Naye hummed. "Uh, that's crazy."

I chuckled.

"Yeah, well, if that means overbearing and overly protective, then maybe, if that's your jam."

"I love your mom!" Venny exclaimed. "She's so pretty and warm... like a sunset."

I felt my chest swell up with pride. She was great and I loved her very much.

"So... how was the party last night?" Venice asked after a while. "I need details."

Looking over to Nairobi, I could tell that she was blushing. I hid my smirk behind my hand, giving her the floor.

"We had such a great time. We met his uncle and practically danced the night away," Nairobi explained, keeping it short and sweet.

"Are you guys official now or…?" Venice raised her eyebrows.

"More than official," I chimed. "Your sister is mine forever, which also means we are family.

"Awesome!" Venice giggled. "Took ya long enough. Honestly, it was taking forever, but I'm glad you guys finally got around to it. Nairobi was—"

"Okay! That's enough sharing for one day!" Naye interrupted, eyes wide. "Anyways, I can't wait to get back to the house. I'm still hungover, and I need to soak."

"We are thirty minutes out, so you should try to get some rest. Don't worry, I'll keep my favorite sister company," I said, giving Venny a little shove, making her laugh.

"Sure."

***

Not long after, both sisters were asleep, which gave me time to give Gabe a heads-up that I was on my way back to town. I was still giddy about last night… and this morning. I felt ready to conquer anything now that I had my queen by my side.

"Wassup, playa?" Gabe greeted. "How was your vacation?"

"Breathing," I replied. "It was everything I expected it to be. Saw my parents. They loved Nairobi and practically adopted Venny as their daughter. I'm just glad that Naye enjoyed herself."

"That's wassup, mane, that's wassup." I could hear his smile over the line. "Well, everything's been quiet... too quiet, actually. Everybody playing their role. Samuel still holed up in them dingy-ass motels on 24th street, and Omar's hiding like a rat."

I hummed. "Well do what you do best, hermano. I ain't nothing but 20 minutes away, tops. We gotta get them before they get us, ya feel me?"

"Heard that, my brotha," he responded. "Peace."

Hanging up, I texted Mrs. Lucille that we were on the way back and to have something prepared for us to eat.

***

The limo pulled around to the front of the house. I sighed in relief. I was glad to be back home.

"Wake up, ladies," I nudged them gently as the driver opened the back door. "We're home."

Naye was the first to stir, pulling herself up into a sitting position. Venice followed suit not long after, rubbing the sleep from her eyes.

"Ugh, my back hurts," she moaned, cracking her lower back. "I can't wait to take a bath."

"Let's get you guys inside so y'all can unwind," I said. "I got the bags."

Getting out first, I let the driver pop the truck so I could gather our things before sending him on his way. Weirdly enough, as we got closer to the house, an eerie feeling settled in my stomach. Just as we reached the porch, I noticed that the door was cracked open like someone had kicked it down. Looking back at both Venice and Nairobi, they had noticed too. I made a motion for them to be quiet and placed the duffle bags on the porch. Reaching under the cushion of the egg chair, I ignored the look Naye gave me and held the gun at arm's length.

"Y'all stay close behind me," I whispered. "When I say run, run, okay?"

"Okay," they whispered.

Pushing the door open, I crept in, ready to shoot. As we got closer to the kitchen, I saw Ms. Lucille's hand resting limp on the tile floor, and quickly redirected us away.

"Y'know, nobody had to die."

I jumped in my skin. The girls did what I wanted to and shrieked. I quickly maneuvered them so that I was shielding their bodies.

"Omar?" Naye said, incredulously. "What are you doing here? How did you find me?"

"Run!" I shouted, shoving them towards the hallway.

"Oh God, do we really have to do this?" Omar exasperated, waving his pistol. "Sammy!"

Samuel came out of nowhere and was able to grab Naye. I tried not to panic and stay calm. At least Venice was able to get out of harm's way, but how was I going to fix this?

"Dad?!" Naye yelled. "What the fuck is this? I told you to leave me alone!"

"What a reunion," Omar smiled. "Sorry to bust your bubble, Robi Gal, but me and your man have business to attend to."

Fuck! I could feel her eyes piercing lasers into my skull.

"What business? Raphael, what is he talking about?"

"I told you that you couldn't trust him, Robi," Samuel said.

"Can someone just tell me what the fuck is going on here?!" she bellowed.

"We go way back," Omar chuckled. "College buddies."

"We were never buddies," I snarled, gun still raised. "I would never hang out with the likes of you, snake."

"Oh please, we both know who the snake really is," Omar poked. "You still haven't told the girl who you really are. Pretending to be this person when really you are just like the rest of us. Low down."

"What do you want?" I asked, ready to end this shit once and for all. "You know why I am here. Samuel tie up the girl," Omar instructed, tossing Samuel some rope. "Oh, don't look like that. He loves her and we need my money. We don't need anyone getting any ideas, like that ole lady we had to put down. Sorry, by the way."

Naye sobbed. "Oh no, Mrs. Lucille."

"I'm sorry, Naye," I said. "I'm going to fix this."

The look she gave me broke my heart. I fucked up big time.

"Place the gun on the floor and kick it towards me," Omar ordered, pointing his gun at me. "Quickly! We don't have all day."

Placing the gun on the floor, I did as I was told and kicked the weapon towards him.

"Lead the way, Mr. Pierre," Omar smirked. "Oh, and Samuel, make sure you watch your daughter… you weren't very good at it before, but I'm sure this will be good practice."

"Fuck you."

Omar laughed, shoving me down the hall.

"You are so lucky, bitch. I hope you know that."

"For someone who has a gun pointed at his spinal cord, you are pretty ballsy," he poked my back with the barrel. "The faster we do this, the quicker I can get out of your hair, and you can get back to playing family."

Entering my office, I could see Venice hiding behind my desk where my safe was. I had to make sure to keep his attention on me. Moving slowly, I made an indistinct motion for her to stay out of sight as I approached her hiding spot.

"How much?" I asked, keeping the conversation going.

"All of it."

Leaning down, I pressed in the combination. Venny looked really scared.

"Ralphie," Venny whispered.

"What's taking so long, Ralph?" Omar called.

Looking up from the safe, I said, "Don't rush me or this shit will lock us both out."

Omar chuckled, shaking his head.

"Venice!" Omar called, readying his weapon. "Come on out, sweetheart, or I will shoot your Ralphie in the head."

"Please don't do that! Here I am," Venice cried out, pushing my legs so she could climb out.

I clenched my jaw, backing away but still kept her behind me.

"Come here, Venice," Omar beckoned. "Let's help Ralphie get my money by you standing next to me."

"O—"

My eyes had to be deceiving me. One moment, I had a gun pointed at me, and the next moment, Naye and Omar were tussling on the ground. The gun had flung to the side. I dove, grabbed it, and aimed it at Omar.

"You bet not do none else, nigga."

17

Nairobi

I tugged at the restraints, wishing I was anywhere but here. The place that had become our sanctuary had become another place of mourning. The man who gave me life looked crazy as he paced back and forth in front of me. His dreads were thinning at the roots, leaving a bald spot in its place. This man—I barely recognized him.

I didn't know where Venice or Raphael was. We were all separated during the struggle, and there was a sinking feeling in my belly.

"Listen, Daddy, please. You don't have to do this. Just let us go, please," I begged, pulling at the restraints. "Where is Venny?"

"I'm sorry, Babygirl. This will all be over once Raphael gives us the money," he rationalized. "After this, we can be a family again. I can introduce you to your sisters and stepmother."

I screamed. "I don't give a fuck about that. Be a family?! This is sick! If you want to fix this, you need to let us go, you sick fuck!"

He growled and backhanded me. I squealed, falling to my side. *Oh God.*

"Typical!" Samuel exclaimed. "This is how you treat your father? Your own blood?"

This man is fucking nuts.

"Either you're out of your mind, or you actually believe that you were a father to me — to us," I glowered. "Last I checked, you left us with nothing! I didn't ask to be here! No one asked for this!"

"You don't think I know I'm a fuck-up?!" Samuel shouted back. "Shit just got too fucked up for me to fix it."

I gulped. "You can still fix this by letting us go."

"I can't," Samuel muttered, retreating a step. "This is my chance to step up and be the father I was supposed to be to you both. Once Omar gets his money, we can all start over. I have to stick to the plan, or I ain't getting my share. Don't you see? I'm doing this for us. We can have a brand-new life after today."

"Do you really think Omar is going to give you anything?" I countered, feeling the rope starting to loosen.

I was barely listening as I looked around for something to defend myself once I got my hands free. I needed to find both Ralph and Venny so we could get the hell out of here. My eyes landed on a glass shard. I could feel my heart racing as I planned my escape.

"I just need you to trust me," Samuel said.

I tuned back in. My hands were finally free, but I made sure to keep them stowed away behind me. If I messed this up, I didn't know what would happen next, so I needed to play this smart.

"Dad, do you know how long I waited for you to come back for us?" I scooted until I was in a seated position. "I prayed every day that you'd show up and fix things. You left us penniless. Mom became a druggie, and I had no choice but to support what was left of our family. I'm sure you already know that Omar enjoyed the clientele I brought in."

"How can I trust you when you left us alone and vulnerable? It's a slap in the face to hear how you've come up in the world, creating a whole other family from scratch. You broke my trust when you walked out on us, and there's nothing you can say or do that will repair any of this."

I could tell that my words cut deep because he felt the need to come closer. I had him right where I wanted him. Close and personal. Holding tightly to the broken glass, I sliced at him with so much force that there was no way he could have avoided it.

An immediate howl filled the space. Wasting no time, I shoved him out of the way and ran in the direction that I saw both Venny, Ralph, and Omar go, hoping to intercept them.

"Nairobi!" Samuel yelled.

I could feel my legs and arms pump faster, leading me through the house. I forced myself to not look back as I pushed myself harder until I could hear Ralph's voice coming from his office. Coming closer, Omar's back was turned to me, but I could see that he was pointing a gun at Ralph, who was shielding Venny with his body.

"Hey!" I yelled, making Omar turn to me.

Without thinking, I shoved him as hard as I could, knocking both him and the gun to the ground. The gun skidded off, leaving me to do as much damage to Omar's face as I could.

"Get the fuck off me, bitch!" Omar growled, striking me in the face and forcing me to the side.

I grunted, blinking away stars that clouded my vision. Raphael immediately jumped into action, grabbing the gun.

"You bet not do none else, nigga," Raphael scowled, pointing the piece at Omar. "Ah, so you really thought this shit was going to go your way? You ain't leaving here alive, and even if you do, ain't no rock you can crawl under where I won't find you."

"Listen, mane, let's talk about this," Omar started, hands raised. "I don't even need the money that bad."

Climbing to my feet, I looked at Raphael. Seeing how well he held his own, everything started coming full circle. I was in love with a kingpin and didn't even know it.

"Venny, go to your—"

"Ralph!"

Everything felt like it was moving in slow motion. There was no stopping Samuel as he fired his gun in Ralph's direction. For a moment, I wish the bullet had struck Ralph, but luck was a rare thing in our lives. I watched, helpless, as two bullets slammed into Venice with such force there was no time to react. Her body hit the floor with a crack.

The air had become still, and it was like my being had left my body as I, too, crumbled to the floor. *My Venny was gone.*

18

Raphael

He shot her. She was going to die, and there was nothing I could do about it. I could barely register what was happening as I turned to look at the bullet dealer. Samuel's pupils were enlarged. He looked high and deranged. He looked between the gun, Omar, and Venice.

"No!" I yelled, dropping the duffle bag and running to Venice's side.

At this point, nothing else mattered. I didn't bother to look up as Omar snatched up the bag of dope and cash, while trying to pull Samuel away from the scene. But he gave up when he realized Samuel wasn't going anywhere.

"It's always nice doing business with you, Raphael," Omar shrugged. "Samuel. Sorry, buddy. Cost of doing business."

He knew he had won, and that there was no standing in his way.

"Ralphie?" Venice called, her eyes glazed with pain. "It hurts, Ralphie."

"I—"

"Just… leave," I snarled at Samuel. "You've done enough."

"I'm sor—"

"Leave!" I shouted, lurching in his direction.

Flinching, Samuel stumbled backward, out of my office, leaving us alone. Turning away from the coward, I cradled Venice in my arms, her blood coating my skin. I fumbled for my cellphone and immediately dialed 911.

"Operator."

"I need help to 3641 Yorkshire St, Greenacres, 33420. There was a break-in and my sister was injured."

"Help is—" I tossed the phone. My mind was clouded. I could barely think straight.

"Take care of my sister, Ralphie," she coughed, blood trickling down her lips. "She…loves…you."

Nairobi. Looking around the office space, I saw her staring in our direction with dead eyes. Her eyes seemed to show no sign of emotion as she looked between Venny's decrepit body and my crestfallen one, but she made no move to come closer. In fact, she looked lost and unsure of herself, as if she had no idea where she was and what was going on around her.

Honestly, I didn't know what to do my damn self. I had vowed to protect these women… and I had failed. What kind of man was I?

Turning back to Venny, I saw her skin had dulled, damp with sweat.

"Don't… cry," she rasped, her pupils becoming glossy with her own tears. "Heaven is… a good place to go."

I didn't even realize that I was crying until what seemed like water had fallen onto her face.

"Venice, stop it, you are going to be just fine," I shushed. "Everything is going to be just fine."

"Hug me, please," she pleaded, tears sliding from the corners of her eyes.

Without hesitation, I pulled her small body closer to my chest and held her… until she took her last breath.

19

Samuel

The image of my daughter lying lifeless on the ground continued to replay in my head over and over again. I could also see Nairobi staring at her sister, eyes lifeless with shock. Her sister was dead. I killed her sister.

Sliding down against the front door, I set the gun down beside me.

How could I be so stupid?

Looking down at my hands, I gagged. Stumbling onto my feet, I threw my body towards the kitchen sink of the dingy motel. Leaning over, I puked my guts out until there was nothing left but bile. Wiping my lips with the back of my hand, I staggered back into what was supposed to be the living space before falling to my knees.

"Stupid! Stupid! Stupid!" I cried, slapping myself in the face. "How could you be so stupid?"

Brring. Brring. Brring.

Fumbling for my phone, I answered on the third ring.

"Honey?" My second wife's voice was soft. She didn't deserve this. "When are you coming home? We miss you. I miss you."

"I'm so sorry, baby," I gurgled, unable to contain myself. "I've fucked up so badly. Do you think God will ever forgive me?"

"Baby, you're scaring me," she said gently. "There's nothing you can do that God won't forgive."

"I don't think what I did can be forgiven," I whispered, picking up the gun.

"Sammy?" she called, her voice tightening. "I don't understand what you are saying. Can you please come home, and we can talk about it?"

"I'm sorry."

Epilogue

S o much has happened in such little time, there was no way to describe how I am feeling. I kept replaying that night in my head, over and over, until all I could think about was revenge.

"Raphael?"

"Hm?"

I was currently at the office, doing some last-minute document filing. It was the holiday season, and there was no way I was doing anything involving paperwork during Christmas. The office would be closed and that would give me time to focus on what really mattered.

It had been almost a year since Venice died, and Nairobi still hadn't regained her memories. Feeling fully responsible for how things played out, I've spent a heavy penny on neurologists, only to be told the same thing: Nairobi's mind has chosen to forget everything as a result of trauma. They warned me not to pressure her into reliving the past — eventually, they said, her memory might return, and when it did, I'd need to help her navigate those fresh memories as if they'd just happened.

So, with that in mind, I've chosen to only tell her what she needs to know to avoid triggering any past experiences.

"Not to rush you or anything, but I'm kind of getting hungry…"

Looking up from the filing cabinet, Naye was lying across the lounge chair, holding her stomach. I chuckled. The person she was now was like night and day in comparison to who she was when we first met. It hurt because I miss that spitfire of a woman.

"C'mon, let's get out of here," I smiled, leaving the folders on the desk.

Hand in hand, we walked to the elevators, hired security trailing behind us. Ever since Venny died, I've worked diligently to make sure she was safe. Despite Omar going into hiding, I knew that his act of violence made me look vulnerable, and that was not a good look for me. It was hard not to feel like there was a target on my back.

As for Samuel… the motel manager found him unresponsive. Dead in the room. The irony.

"Are you okay?" Nairobi peered up at me. "You shouldn't grind your teeth; you'll have nubs for choppers."

"I don't remember you being this funny," I laughed.

"I don't remember either," she winked, letting me guide her out of the elevator. "I've accepted the idea of never remembering and honestly I'm ready to reinvent myself."

I winced.

"I guess so…" I trailed off. "Is there anything you want to know? Anything been bothering you?"

She hummed thoughtfully, climbing into the limo. Getting in behind her, I felt the door close behind us.

"Well… there is this one thing," she mumbled, playing with her fingers. "The name Omar keeps popping into my head. His face is fuzzy. There's so much blood, and I keep seeing this girl, but I don't know who she is. The image is… really scary, honestly. It makes me question who was I, y'know?"

"I can understand how scary this is," I exhaled slowly. "But don't worry. I will make this right."

"How?" she bristled. "The doctors don't think I'll ever regain my memories. What can you possibly do to fix this?"

"I will make sure the person who did this to you pays for his mistakes."